Aud

DANGER
in the Cove

Scripture Union

For Alice and Emily with my love

By the same author:
Hidden Prizes – Impressions series

© Audrey Constant 1996

First published 1996

Scripture Union, 207–209 Queensway, Bletchley,
Milton Keynes, MK2 2EB, England.

ISBN 1 85999 037 1

All rights reserved. No part of this publication may
be reproduced, stored in a retrieval system, or
transmitted, in any form or by any means, electronic,
mechanical, photocopying, recording or otherwise,
without the prior permission of Scripture Union.

The right of Audrey Constant to be identified as
author of this work has been asserted by her in
accordance with the Copyright, Designs and Patents
Act 1988.

British Library Cataloguing-in-Publication Data.
A catalogue record of this book is available from the
British Library.

Printed and bound in Great Britain by Cox & Wyman
Ltd, Reading.

Chapter one

Bryn first noticed the boy and his father on the ferry as it ploughed its way through choppy seas between the Isles of Scilly.

They were sitting opposite him. Both were fair and heavily built. The boy was about sixteen but it was his eyes that struck Bryn. They were a piercing green.

Bryn could only hear some of their conversation above the noise of the engine but they were arguing. He gathered it had something to do with deep-sea diving. The boy seemed to be trying to persuade his father to let him have a go but he was brushed aside.

'I said you could come with us but we've got a job to do and there's no time to hang about. This time it isn't practice. It's for real and it's going to be dangerous.'

'But I want to help. If you gave me a chance, Dad, I could be just as good as the others.'

His father was getting impatient and raised his voice so that Bryn could easily hear and, by now, he was listening hard. What was it that was so dangerous and they were going to do for real?

'That's enough, Mark. I warned you if I let you

come along on this trip you'd have to amuse yourself at least part of the time and that's final. It's no good going on about it.'

Bryn watched the colour in his face rise as the son turned away, biting his lip and, for a moment, he saw anger in his eyes as he looked straight across at Bryn.

There was no time for further words. The ferry was slowing down and when Bryn looked ahead he saw that it was nosing its way alongside the quay. Father and son were already pushing past the other passengers and Bryn saw them leap off the ferry almost before she was tied up. They seemed to know their way about but then St Agnes was only a small island and if you lived here Bryn reckoned you would get to know it pretty well.

Then his thoughts were interrupted by his Aunt Millie who had been sheltering in the cabin.

'This is where we get off. Got everything?'

He checked to see that his binoculars were still safely round his neck. Then he slung his rucksack over his shoulders and, picking up his holdall, followed her off the ferry.

'We'll have to walk,' she said. 'The distances aren't great here and no one owns a car except the builder and the butcher, folk who need them for their work. You'll soon get used to it.'

They took the narrow tarmac road which led from the harbour and ran over the ridge of the island. It was steep, and Bryn was hot and exhausted. It had taken them all day to get here from London, and he was glad when at last his aunt stopped in front of a cottage with a yellow door.

'Here we are,' she said, smiling at him. 'Come on in.'

4

Bryn stepped into a cool cottage with low ceilings and small windows. It took a moment or two before his eyes adjusted to the light and he saw a boy coming through from the kitchen. He was older and taller than Bryn, who was on the small side and darker than his cousin.

'Remember Sam?' asked his aunt. 'It's some years since you two met.' Sam nodded.

'Hullo,' he said. 'I didn't know you were bringing Bryn back with you.'

'It was arranged at the last moment,' explained his aunt. 'The twins had gone off to a summer camp and Bryn was at a loose end so I persuaded his mother to let him come back with me. I hope now he's here you'll spend a bit of time with him, Sam. He's keen on birds.'

'Plenty of them about,' said Sam. 'I'm going down to the fishing harbour now to help Dad.' He turned to Bryn. 'Want to come?'

Aunt Millie answered for him. 'Not yet. He can come on down later. I'm sure you could do with a bite to eat first, Bryn. Before you go, Sam, take him upstairs. I've made up the bed in the small back room.'

She went into the kitchen, and Bryn followed his cousin up the narrow wooden stairway to a tiny room where there was just space for a bed, a small table and a chest of drawers.

'How long are you staying?' asked Sam, dropping Bryn's holdall on to the bed.

'I'm not sure,' said Bryn. 'About two weeks, I think. Mum's coming to fetch me. She's taking a couple of days off work.'

Sam paused at the door on his way out. 'Hope you won't be bored here by yourself. You'll find it pretty quiet after London.'

'I won't,' said Bryn. 'I really wanted to come. Could we go bird-watching some time?'

'I can't promise. I'm pretty busy just now, helping Dad with the fishing boats, but you'll see them around anyway. There are a lot over on Annet Island but you'd have to get a boat there.'

'I expect I'll discover them,' said Bryn.

'You'll find those useful.' Sam nodded towards the binoculars which Bryn clutched in his hand. 'Where did you get them? You can't have much use for them in London, surely?'

'Mum gave them to me for my birthday two days ago. She promised I could have a pair when I was eleven. I used to go to the common with Dad. We saw quite a lot of birds there.'

'You'll find they're different here,' said Sam. 'Guillemots, razorbills, that sort of thing. Puffins, if you're lucky.'

'Great!' said Bryn. 'I'll be able to build up my list.'

'I don't bother about that sort of thing myself. Take birds for granted. See them all the time. Look, I've got to go now. See you later.'

Bryn heard him running down the stairs. He went over to the window. The cottage was one in a row and at the bottom of the garden a gate opened on to a path which led down to the sea. Far beyond were clusters of islands. He couldn't wait to get out there and explore. It didn't worry him much if he had to do it on his own. He was used to that and, besides, he would stand a better chance of seeing something rare. If he was lucky, he might even spot a seal. He had never seen one before, not in real life anyway.

Downstairs, Aunt Millie had laid the table. It hadn't taken her long to make a plate of sandwiches and there was a chocolate cake and a pot of tea. Bryn was ravenous.

'You'll probably find Sam and your uncle down at the fishing harbour,' she said. 'There's a short cut through the garden gate but why don't you walk through the village and have a look round?'

'Can I go anywhere?' asked Bryn.

'Of course. You can't come to any harm so long as you don't get close to the cliffs.'

He set off, taking a path that led past the church and came down to a small quay where the fishing boats were moored. There were a few people about, fishermen mending their nets and one or two tourists in sun-tops and shorts, looking a bright shade of red. He was glad he wasn't one of them. He felt as though he belonged here already.

He couldn't see Sam anywhere. He doubted whether he'd even recognise his uncle. It was such a long time since he'd seen him. He crossed a field and paused to watch some boys kicking a ball about. There was an older lad among them and Bryn immediately recognised him as the one he had seen on the ferry. He seemed to be in charge of the game and kicked the ball in all directions, then sent the younger ones off to collect it.

There was one boy in particular that he picked on. He stood by himself and, although he was part of the game, he was slow to react and suddenly a hard ball hit him fair and square on his chest, nearly knocking him over. The ball went rolling down the hill towards the sea.

'Wake up, you idiot!'

The younger boys sniggered, unaware that the

boy seemed to be having trouble breathing.

'You missed it. You get it,' shouted the leader.

Bryn ran down the field and retrieved the ball and tossed it back to the group.

'You all right?' he asked the boy as he passed.

The boy smiled. 'Thanks. I'm OK now. Think I've had enough though.' He turned and walked off the field.

Bryn was about to continue on his way along the cliff path when a loud voice followed him.

'Hey you! He didn't ask for your help. He can get his own ball.'

Bryn stopped to answer. 'He didn't look well,' he said, 'so I got it for him.'

'You'd do better to mind your own business!'

Bryn went on without looking back. He could hear the boys laughing at him but he wasn't going to get involved. But he was glad he had stood up for the boy. He had looked badly shaken.

Presently the path dropped down towards a rocky cove. Seaweed made the rocks slippery here and he moved with care. Scrambling down, he eventually reached the beach. The tide was out, leaving pools between the rocks in which small crabs and urchins lived. Bryn squatted down, fascinated by all the creatures crawling about.

This was a fantastic place. It was easy to believe all those stories his mother had told him about these islands. He had wondered why they were called Scilly and thought it might be something to do with the people who lived here. Whatever, it seemed a place where all kinds of exciting things could happen.

Hang on! What was that out there? As he watched, a small black head appeared on the surface of the water. Was it really a seal or did his eyes deceive him? He stood up and began to whistle softly. He'd heard somewhere that seals like music. It must be true; it was coming slowly towards him. Then suddenly, without warning, it dived and disappeared from sight. He waited for ages, hoping for another glimpse, but it had gone.

Disappointed, Bryn sighed and turned for home. Tomorrow he'd be back. Once the seal got used to him and understood that he meant it no harm, he might even be able to tame it.

By the time he reached the cottage his uncle and Sam had returned and were sitting down at the long wooden table in the kitchen waiting for supper. Bryn vaguely remembered his uncle now. He looked like a fisherman with his broad shoulders and thick grey hair and weather-beaten face.

He smiled. 'Hullo, Bryn. Welcome to St Agnes.'

'Thanks,' said Bryn, joining them at the table. Aunt Millie put a home-baked pie in front of them and served out equal portions with fresh vegtables from the garden.

'So, what do you want to do while you're here?' asked Uncle Frank, picking up his knife and fork.

'I'd like to have a look for some birds,' said Bryn.

'We can promise you plenty of those. Shags and cormorants are common enough and you might even see a shearwater.'

'I think I can identify them,' said Bryn eagerly. 'I looked them up in my book before I came.'

'I can see you're a serious ornithologist,' said his uncle.

'I saw a few just now,' said Bryn, eagerly. 'And a seal. It came quite close. Are there many here?'

'Plenty. Some say too many.'

'They're on the increase,' said Sam. 'Most of the fishermen are complaining that the seals are eating all the fish.'

'Maybe,' said Uncle Frank, 'but I reckon they have as much right to their food as we do. Live and let live, I say.'

'Are we going fishing tomorrow?' asked Sam.

'Yes,' said his father. 'Once I've got the mackerel lines sorted out. Maybe Bryn would like to come?'

'Can I really?' said Bryn. He hadn't expected to go on a fishing trip quite so soon.

'You can,' said his uncle. 'But it's an early start. I'll call you at six.'

'Then you'll need a good night's sleep,' said Aunt Millie. 'How about bed?'

But, upstairs, Bryn was far too excited to sleep. He lay listening to the muffled sound of the waves breaking on the cliffs below his window and the wind whistling round the cottage.

It was so wild here, so different from the little terraced house in the suburbs of London where he lived and nothing much ever happened. Not since his dad left them a year ago. The twins rarely included him in their activities and his mum always wanted to know where he was going. She seemed scared to let him out of her sight.

But here it looked as though he would have all the freedom he wanted. In a way, it was a bit scary but of one thing he was sure. It was going to be the most exciting holiday he'd ever had.

Chapter two

Bryn was woken by a knock on his door and, springing out of bed, he pulled on his jeans and a shirt and ran downstairs. His uncle and aunt were already at breakfast.

'We always make an early start,' said Aunt Millie. 'Fishermen work all hours, often through the night, but you don't have to get up at this time every day.'

'Where's Sam?' asked Bryn.

'He's gone on down to get the boat ready,' said Uncle Frank. 'Just as soon as you've finished your cornflakes we'll go.'

Bryn gulped them down, picked up a pullover and was ready.

'The door's always open,' said his aunt. 'You can get in any time but I might not be here.'

Down at the harbour Sam was already in *Seafarer* sorting out the mackerel lines. He reached out a hand to help Bryn in and told him where to sit. It was horribly close to the water. Bryn had expected something like the ferry that had brought him here but this boat was far smaller and rocked dangerously. Once his father was aboard, Sam started up the engine and, the next moment, *Seafarer* was heading out to sea.

'That's Annet Island out there.' Uncle Frank pointed to an island across the channel about a mile away. 'It's a bird sanctuary and no one is allowed to land there without permission.'

'Do you have permission?' asked Bryn.

'Yes, but if I wanted to take you I would have to ask a warden. They don't allow people there when the birds are nesting or the seals are breeding.'

'What about the other islands?' asked Bryn.

'Nothing much on them,' said Sam. 'Except a lighthouse, then nothing more till America.'

Bryn considered this. All that sea between him and America!

They were well away from the harbour now, on the open sea, and Uncle Frank threw the lines overboard. Within a few minutes they pulled in four silvery fish and landed them inside the boat.

Bryn watched Sam grab the fish, and tried not to flinch as Sam pulled the hooks out of their mouths before banging them on the head with a piece of wood. He tossed them into a bucket where they writhed for a few more moments before lying still.

'Nerves,' said Sam, looking across to Bryn. 'They're dead. It's only their nerves reacting.'

Bryn looked away. He was feeling a bit sick, though whether it was the movement of the boat or the writhing fish he wasn't sure.

In no time at all they had three large buckets full of dead mackerel and Uncle Frank declared that it was enough for one morning. Sam turned the boat towards a channel between some islands and pointed her towards the harbour.

'Look,' he said, 'there's a launch over there. I

wonder what they're up to?' Bryn could just see it, half hidden by islands.

'Most likely fishing without permission,' said Uncle Frank.

'Let me have your binoculars for a moment, Bryn.' Sam reached out for them and focused on the launch.

'Those men on board are wearing wet suits,' he said. 'That means they're diving. I wonder if they're after wrecks.'

'Not without permission. They'd have the law on them,' said Uncle Frank.

'Are they looking for treasure?' asked Bryn, suddenly interested.

'They'd only find treasure on the very old wrecks,' said his uncle, 'and most of that's been taken already or dispersed by strong currents.'

'If you find it can you keep it?' asked Bryn.

'Course not,' said Sam. 'You have to report it.'

'All treasure has to be returned to its rightful owner which might be the insurance company or the shipping company or the navy if it's a naval ship,' Uncle Frank explained. 'If it isn't claimed, the state is entitled to it. In any case, you have to have special permission to dive on to a wreck, added to which it is highly dangerous. So, all in all it's hardly worth doing.'

'What shall we do about them then?' asked Sam.

'Leave them to it. I don't expect they're going deep. That's a specialised job. More likely they're just taking a look at the rocks round there.'

Bryn didn't say anything. He was wondering if they had anything to do with the two he'd seen on the ferry the day before. Perhaps this was what they had been talking about. Anyway, it didn't concern him and Uncle Frank didn't seem unduly worried.

When they got back and Bryn scrambled on to the quay he could still feel the movement of the boat. Uncle Frank and Sam tipped the mackerel into a container which was then loaded on to a bigger boat.

'Think you'll be able to amuse yourself for a while, Bryn? We've got to get this stuff away. We'll see you later.'

Bryn was quite happy to be on his own for a while. He thought he might look for the seal.

He took the path that led up the hill. He could see for miles from here. The sea was incredibly blue and calm and dotted with islands. Over there he could see Annet. He wondered if anyone lived there. Perhaps a warden? But he could see no houses. In fact, it looked quite desolate. He'd have to ask his uncle if he would take him one day. It must be a great place for birds. Then, taking the steep path, he went down to the sea.

The tide was out and below him lay a sandy beach dotted with rocks. The only sound was of waves breaking on the shore and overhead the cry of the gulls. He sat down to watch and began to feel quite drowsy.

Suddenly he was alert. Surely that was the seal again and it was swimming towards him. Bryn took off his shoes and ran to the edge of the water. The seal stayed there watching him. It was a dark grey colour with a sleek head and he could see its big sad eyes and whiskers. He began talking to it in a low voice, trying to persuade it to come closer. If he could tame it, it might allow him to swim with it. He was a good swimmer.

He was about to go deeper into the water when a stone flew over his head and dropped just short of the seal which immediately disappeared. When Bryn spun round to see who was standing behind him, a sudden spasm of fear swept through him.

'What are you doing?' demanded Bryn, beside himself with anger.

'Trying to hit him. You don't want to encourage those things. They do a lot of damage.'

'They don't,' said Bryn, coming out of the water. 'They've as much right as you and me to be there.'

'What do you know?' The boy looked at Bryn closely. 'You don't live here do you? I saw you coming over on the ferry yesterday, didn't I?'

'I'm staying with my uncle here and he says seals are OK.'

'They eat fish. Ask any proper fisherman and he'll tell you.'

Bryn looked into the piercing green eyes and found it hard to stand his ground. There was something about this boy that scared him.

'There are plenty of fish,' Bryn ventured. 'My uncle says so.'

'Your uncle! Who's he, anyway?'

'His name's Frank Cox. He's a fisherman and he's lived here all his life. He knows more about seals than most people.' Bryn reckoned this must be true. 'He's out fishing now and will be back at any moment. I went out this morning but I came to find that seal and now you've driven it away.'

The boy jumped down from a high rock and landed behind Bryn, blocking the path up the cliff. He towered over him and Bryn looked quickly round to see if there was an escape route but, apart from scrambling over high rocks, there was no other way up the cliff. Nor was there anyone else in sight. Bryn took a grip of himself. He wasn't going to be intimidated by this bully.

The boy looked straight at him. 'Look,' he said. 'I'm going to give you some friendly advice. I know this island and it can be dangerous. You'd do well to keep to the beaches where everyone else swims if you don't want to find yourself in trouble.'

'What do you know about it?' asked Bryn. 'Who are you, anyway?'

'My name's Tyler. Mark Tyler. I'm just warning you, that's all.'

More likely he wanted to keep the best places for himself, thought Bryn. His anger gave him courage. 'Anyway, what right have you got to tell me where I can go?'

Mark shrugged. 'It's up to you. If you're wise you'll take advice from someone who knows.'

It occurred to Bryn that Tyler could be the son of a fisherman himself. He seemed to know what he was talking about. He thought he'd better try and find out more about him so that he could check with Uncle Frank.

'Do you live here?' he asked.

'On and off. We're here for the summer.' Mark picked up another stone and threw it at random into the water. Bryn ignored it. He knew Tyler was trying to provoke him.

He glanced towards the water. The seal had gone for good. It was no use staying here but how was he to get past? Mark was still blocking the path. There was only one way and he had to try it. Picking up his shoes, he pushed his way past. To his surprise, Mark did not try to stop him and Bryn carried on up the hill.

16

Chapter three

When Bryn got back he found the front door open. He went through to the garden and flung himself down in the shade. The cat came and curled herself against him, purring, and he stroked her absentmindedly. He could have been so happy here if it hadn't been for Mark Tyler. He just hoped that he wasn't going to pop up every time he went to look for seals. It would ruin everything.

He must have dropped off to sleep because Uncle Frank's voice woke him. 'Anyone at home?'

Bryn got up and went to find him.

'Let's see what we've got for lunch,' his uncle went on. 'Your aunt leaves something in the fridge when she's out.' He poked around and brought out a salad and some cheese. 'There now, help yourself.'

Bryn found he was hungry after all. 'I saw the seal again this morning,' he said, tucking in. 'It was swimming straight towards me and then a boy threw a stone at it and it disappeared.'

'Silly of him,' said Uncle Frank. 'Did you tell him off?'

'Sort of. Actually he was telling me off for being there. Was he allowed to do that?'

Uncle Frank shook his head. 'Certainly not,' he said. 'I hope you ignored him. People can come and go as they please on this island. What was he doing there anyway?'

'Staying here for the summer. He said his name's Mark Tyler. I saw him on the ferry coming over here.'

'Never heard of him. Sounds an unpleasant character. One of those people who thinks he owns the place.'

'He said he knows the island well and he went on about seals doing a lot of damage. I told him it wasn't true.'

'Quite right.' Uncle Frank had finished his lunch. He pushed back his chair and got up. 'Now, I've got work to do. I'm afraid you'll have to amuse yourself this afternoon. I must apologise for Sam. He went off crabbing with a friend.'

'I'm OK,' said Bryn. 'I'll go and have another look for that seal.'

He made his way down the cliff path, bracing himself against the loose stones. When he reached the bottom he waited a long time, looking across the water, searching for the seal. He had been so certain that it would be there waiting for him. But then he had to be realistic. It was a wild creature and by now it might be miles away. Or perhaps in the next cove?

He sized up the situation. The tide was coming in and he would have to negotiate those rocks. Would he be able to get back? The only way to find out was to try.

It took quite a time but eventually he got to a spot where he could see round the promontory.

And there, on a rock just above the water, lay the seal, basking in the sun.

It was big, about three feet long, and it must have been asleep for its eyes were closed. As Bryn crept closer he could see its whiskers twitching. Its grey coat was short and smooth, like velvet. On each of its flippers were five shiny black nails.

He could almost touch it now. As he crept towards it, a small rowing boat came into sight with a man pulling at the oars. With him was a boy about Bryn's own age.

Bryn remained where he was, only a few yards from the seal, hoping that they would continue on their way but they swung round into the cove. The seal awoke and, alarmed to see Bryn so close, heaved itself to the edge of the rock and plopped into the water.

It wasn't until the boat slid into the narrow channel between the rocks that Bryn recognised the boy he had seen on the football pitch.

The man got out of the boat and secured it to an iron stake sunk into a rock. He looked to be in his forties. The lower part of his face was covered with a beard and his hair could only be described as shaggy. He had deep-set brown eyes which looked at Bryn in a friendly manner.

'Hi there,' he said. 'I didn't expect to find anyone here.'

'I came over the rocks,' said Bryn.

'I haven't seen you about before, have I?'

'I've only just come,' said Bryn. 'I'm staying with my uncle.'

'Then I expect I know him. Let me introduce myself. I'm Murray. I've been around for some time so most of the folk know me. And this is my

19

son, Pete. Now, suppose you tell us who you are.'

'Bryn, that's short for Bryan. I like it better. I came here to look for the seal.'

'Then I'm glad you found her,' said Murray.

Bryn was intrigued. 'Do you know her then?' he asked.

'Of course I know her. I looked after her when she was a pup. Got knocked about on the rocks, she did, in some nasty weather. She was with me for a month, then I let her go, but she's never forgotten me. She goes off for a while, then back she comes. One day she'll be gone for good. That's the way of seals.'

This man seemed to know a lot about them. In spite of his disappointment at being disturbed just when he was about to touch the seal, Bryn thought he might learn something from him.

'I wish I knew more about them,' he said.

Murray was looking round the rocks and into all the crevices.

'Want to make sure there aren't any young ones in difficulties,' he said. 'It cut up a bit rough last night. I take any injured ones to a special place I've made. Seal pups leave their mothers when they're only a few weeks old and have to fend for themselves. We have quite a lot of casualties.'

'Are you looking after some now?' asked Bryn.

'I've just been to feed them. They need to eat several times a day.'

'Where are they?' asked Bryn.

'In a special enclosure I've made for them,' Murray explained. 'I have to keep it secret or there'd be all sorts of people going there, upsetting them.'

'Could I see them?' asked Bryn.

'We could take him there now, couldn't we?' Pete spoke up for the first time.

His father shook his head. 'No. The food's finished. Another time perhaps.' He turned to Bryn. 'How are you getting back? Want a lift?'

Bryn looked at the boat. It was small, even smaller than Uncle Frank's and the water looked awfully deep. Outside the cove, he could hear the waves crashing against the rocks.

'I don't think so, thank you,' he said. 'I'll go back the way I came.' But even as he looked, the water was sweeping over the rocks.

Murray grinned. 'You'll be all right with us. We come here every day.'

It seemed the only alternative. 'All right then,' said Bryn. 'Thanks.'

Murray helped him into the boat and unhooked the rope. It rocked dangerously but as soon as they were out in the channel, well clear of the rocks, Murray started up the engine and they went along steadily. Bryn found he was getting used to the sea. In fact he quite enjoyed the sensation of the boat cutting through the water and the wind blowing about his face.

'Are you in the habit of wandering around by yourself?' Murray asked presently.

'When my cousin's busy,' said Bryn. 'He's older than me and he helps my uncle.'

'What's your uncle's name?' asked Murray.

'Cox. Frank Cox. He's a fisherman.'

'I know him well,' said Murray. 'I expect he's told you to keep away from the cliffs. It's a different matter if you've been raised here. You get to know where it's safe, but for a newcomer it can be dangerous.'

He didn't say any more and concentrated on steering the boat between the ugly rocks which protruded along the coast. Bryn glanced towards Pete. He was trailing his hand in the water and caught his eye.

'Want to see our bird hospital?' asked Pete.

'Could I?' asked Bryn eagerly. 'Where is it?'

'At the cottage. Dad made an aviary for injured birds. We've got an owl with a broken wing. It's better now but it doesn't want to fly away.'

'When can I come?' asked Bryn.

'Tomorrow, if you like. I'm not allowed to handle the birds myself because of my asthma, but I can show them to you.'

Murray swung the boat into the harbour. 'Here we are,' he said. 'You two can jump out now.'

Bryn waited as Pete helped his father to tie up the boat. Not far away Uncle Frank was working on his fishing lines and Bryn wandered over.

'Hullo, Bryn. Sam was looking for you. He's got some crabs over there. Why don't you go over and have a look?'

Sam was peering into a bucket where a pile of small crabs were struggling to get out. With him was Mark Tyler.

'Where've you been?' asked Sam.

'With Murray. He brought me back in his boat.'

'See any seals?' enquired Sam.

'One. Murray's got a special place where he looks after the sick ones.' Bryn felt quite important being the bearer of news that even Sam didn't know about. 'He said he'd take me along to see them some time.'

'I'd like to have a look at them,' said Sam. 'Think he'd take us along?'

Bryn shrugged, suddenly aware that he might have said too much. 'I dunno,' he said. 'They're nervous creatures and Murray doesn't like people going there.'

'Go and ask him, Bryn,' his cousin went on. 'Find out when he's going again.'

'Why bother?' interrupted Mark. 'We don't have to wait for him. I've got the use of my dad's dinghy. We can see if we can spot them for ourselves. What do you say, Sam?'

'Great,' said Sam, enthusiastically.

'Any idea where he keeps them?' Mark asked.

'No,' said Bryn. He ought to warn Sam about Mark. 'I'm going on home. Are you coming?'

'In a minute,' said Sam.

Bryn wandered off and waited for Sam at the top of the hill.

'Mark Tyler was throwing stones at a seal yesterday,' Bryn said when Sam caught him up. 'He doesn't like them.'

'He's OK,' said Sam. 'He's crazy about deep-sea diving. Does a lot of it.'

'By himself?' asked Bryn.

'Don't be daft,' said Sam. 'You can't do that sort of thing on your own. It's very dangerous and you have to know what you're doing. He goes out with his father. They've got a big launch and a crew. He said he might take me along some time.'

'Would you be allowed?' asked Bryn.

'Why not? Dad wouldn't mind. Anyway it's a chance to learn more about it.' He frowned and kicked a stone along the path. Then, after a moment, he said, 'As a matter of fact, I like Mark. I want to see more of him.'

Chapter four

'Murray says he'll take you to see the seals tomorrow if you go along to his cottage, Bryn,' said Uncle Frank at supper-time. 'You'll find it at the end of Carter's Lane.'

'I'd like to come too,' said Sam.

'Not this time.' Uncle Frank was firm. 'The invitation is for Bryn.'

'Ask him if I can come next time then,' said Sam, turning to Bryn.

Bryn said nothing. If Sam found out where the seals were, he would tell Mark.

'There might not be room in his boat,' he said finally.

Sam shrugged. 'Doesn't matter. It will be more fun to go with Mark anyway.'

Bryn had no difficulty in finding the cottage. It was old with white-washed walls and small latticed windows, standing in a wild-looking garden. The front door stood wide open and the next moment Murray's tall figure appeared.

'Come on in,' he said. 'Like a cold drink?'

'Yes please,' said Bryn.

He looked about him. The interior of the tiny cottage was blissfully cool after the heat outside.

The stone floor was covered with rugs and the ceiling was so low that it just cleared Murray's head. Bookcases lined the walls and a Bible lay open on the table. On the wall hung a large map of the Scilly Isles. Bryn was fascinated by maps and went to have a look at it. He identified St Agnes and Annet and pinpointed the lane that led to Pete's cottage.

'Interested?' asked Murray, coming to join him.

'Yes,' said Bryn. 'What funny names. Brothers and Hellweathers and those rocks near the lighthouse. Who names them?'

Murray shrugged. 'Local people I expect. They've been known by those names for centuries and eventually they found their way on to the maps.'

A woman came in from the kitchen with a jug of fresh fruit juice. She was plump with fair curly hair and smiled happily at Bryn. 'Welcome,' she said, pouring out three glasses and setting them on the table. 'I'm Pete's mother but most folk know me as Maizie. So, you've come to see his aviary, have you? He's out there now.'

'And to see the seals,' said Bryn hopefully, with a glance towards Murray.

'Sure,' said Murray. 'When Pete's finished feeding the birds, we'll be off.' Murray picked up his pipe and filled it. 'So what do you think of our island?'

'It's a wonderful place,' said Bryn with enthusiasm.

'Different from London?' suggested Maizie.

'I hate London,' said Bryn.

'I once lived in London,' said Murray. 'Used to work there.'

'Why did you leave?' asked Bryn.

'I was a school teacher. We always used to come here for the holidays.'

'But when Pete was so ill with asthma,' broke in Maizie, 'and he needed good clean air, we decided to come and live in the islands.'

'Don't you ever leave?'

'Rarely, except when Pete has to go over to the mainland for treatment.' Maizie picked up the tray and returned to the kitchen.

'What about you, Bryn?' asked Murray. 'Have you got a family?'

Bryn was silent for a moment. He didn't like talking about his family – not since his dad left. It didn't feel like a family any more. He glanced at Murray. He would like to tell him about it but he wasn't sure. It still hurt too much.

Murray smiled at him. 'Brother and sister perhaps?'

'Yes, twins,' said Bryn. 'And my mum. She's working.'

'Ah, yes,' said Murray.

'Then my dad.' He paused and then rushed on. 'My dad left last year. He found someone he liked better than us.'

He suddenly felt like crying but managed to hold back the tears.

Murray gave him time, then he said quietly, 'That does sometimes happen, Bryn, and it hurts very much.'

'I hate him,' Bryn burst out.

Murray was about to answer when Pete came in.

'Didn't know you were here,' he said to Bryn, picking up his juice and drinking it in one go. 'Want to see the birds?'

26

Murray went to the door. 'I'll go down to the harbour and get the mackerel,' he said. 'You two can come on down later.'

Bryn followed Pete to the end of the garden where there was a big aviary, room enough for a number of birds to perch on the tree stumps and fly about.

'Dad built it,' said Pete. 'We get a lot of injured birds here. That owl got blown off course. It was exhausted and had a broken wing. I let him out but he always comes back. That one over there is an oystercatcher. A fisherman brought him here. He'd picked up some oil somewhere.'

'How long will you keep them here?' asked Bryn.

'Depends how badly they're hurt. See that hut over there?' Pete looked towards a shack half covered with ivy. 'Dad keeps the baby seals there if they're sick or injured.'

'I wish I could rig up something like this at home for injured birds,' said Bryn.

'But you live in London. You wouldn't have much use for it there, would you?'

'Maybe not,' said Bryn wistfully.

'Are you all right?' asked Pete. 'You look kind of sad.'

'I'm OK,' said Bryn. 'I like your dad.'

'He's the best dad in the world,' said Pete.

'You're lucky,' said Bryn, overwhelmed by his loss.

'By the way,' said Pete, suddenly feeling shy, 'thanks for getting that ball for me the other evening. I can't run too far 'cos I have trouble with my breathing.'

'Your mum said you had asthma and came here

27

to live so that you'd get better.'

'I won't ever get better,' said Pete. He was silent for a moment, then went on slowly, 'I used to be angry and unhappy because I was ill and couldn't do all the things my friends did. But Dad said that it isn't what happens to us that's important, it's how we handle it that matters. We have to ask Jesus to help us through difficult times. When I tried that I felt much better. It's like having a special friend helping you.'

This was quite a new idea to Bryn. He'd never thought much about Jesus.

'How can you have a friend you can't see?' he asked. 'A friend is someone you can get angry with, laugh with, have fun with.'

'I don't need to see him,' said Pete. 'I just know he's there. Sometimes I even argue with him but I don't think he minds that. I know he puts up with me whatever I'm like. Not many friends are like that, are they?'

'P'raps not,' said Bryn. He was thinking of his father. He wondered if Jesus could help him over his awful feeling of anger. He didn't really believe that he could. No one could.

'Jesus stands by us no matter what,' said Pete. He closed the aviary door. 'Come on. I think we'd better go. Dad will be waiting for us.'

They reached the harbour as Murray came striding along the quayside with a bucket full of mackerel. He unhitched the boat, pulled the starter and the engine sprang to life. The next moment they were off.

Murray nosed the boat along, keeping close to the shore. The beaches were deserted here and tables of submerged rock broke the swell, throwing up cascades of white spray. They passed the place where the cliff path came steeply down to the shore and the cove where yesterday they had seen the seal. There was no sign of her today.

Presently Murray turned into another cove surrounded by high cliffs and switched off the engine.

'Point Witcher,' he said, picking up the oars and rowing towards a sandy beach. With a final pull, the boat grounded and, reaching for the bucket, Murray jumped ashore, leaving the boys to follow.

Bryn scrambled out and looked up at the cliff. No one could reach the cove that way. It seemed that the only way was by boat. The cliff plunged steeply towards the rocks below and opened to form the entrance to a small cave. In front of it, Murray had erected a strong linked wire fence, kept in place by metal stakes. The seals had a natural area of sand and rocks, yet they could not escape.

They had heard Murray and were gathering by the entrance, grunting with pleasure.

'You two wait here,' said Murray, going in with the bucket. Bryn watched as he threw each seal in turn a small mackerel which it caught and swallowed whole. There were seven of them, varying in size. Some were smaller and still had their baby coats, soft and creamy coloured, but others had already grown their new, dark grey adult skins. One had a damaged flipper, another a long gash on its side which was healing. They clambered round Murray using their strong flippers to support their heavy bodies.

When they had finished their meal, Murray checked each one carefully and then came out, securing the entrance firmly behind him.

'A couple of the older ones can be released soon,' he said. 'If they're kept too long in captivity they'll find it hard to adapt to freedom.'

'Where did they come from?' asked Bryn.

'Fishermen bring them to me or I find them round the coast. They were all injured in some way or other. A couple came from Annet. They'd been attacked by the gulls when they were quite small.'

'They're not afraid of you,' said Bryn.

'They were at first. Terrified. You have to build up their trust and then they are quite affectionate and don't want to let you out of their sight. Sally, the one you saw yesterday, she was like that.'

'I wish I could have one as a pet,' said Bryn.

'You couldn't take it home,' said Pete. 'They're wild creatures and they can't live without the sea. It would be cruel to keep them in captivity.'

'Could I touch one?'

'Best let them get used to you,' said Murray. 'They could give you a nasty bite.'

'I saw a boy throwing stones at Sally the other day,' said Bryn. "I don't know how he could.'

'Some people are like that,' said Murray, picking up the empty bucket. 'They're sick.'

Bryn turned to Pete. 'Actually it was the same boy who was playing football with you the other evening. His name's Mark Tyler.'

'He's here on holiday,' said Pete. 'We were having quite a decent game when he joined in and started kicking the ball all over the place.'

'Always people like that around,' said Murray. 'His bark's probably worse than his bite.'

As Bryn followed them back to the boat he heard the sound of a motor and, the next moment, a launch came into view. He focused his binoculars on the deck where some men stood looking towards the cove. One was younger than the others.

Bryn caught up with Pete. 'That's Mark Tyler,' he said. 'Must be his father's launch.' He lowered his glasses, searching for the name on the hull. '*The Gannet*,' he read out.

Murray waited until the launch was well on its way before he left the cove.

'They're making for Annet,' he said. 'I don't like it. They'll disturb the wildlife.'

'Can't you stop them?' asked Bryn.

'Not unless they try to land. No one is allowed to land there, only wardens. It's a bird sanctuary.'

'What would happen if they did?'

'They'd be turned off but it's not always easy to spot them. On the far side the rocks are very dangerous as plenty of ships have found to their cost. If anyone ventures there they can't be seen. We try to keep a check on Annet but we don't always know what's going on out there.'

That evening, at supper, Sam asked Bryn if he had seen the seals.

'Yes,' said Bryn, suddenly busy with his pudding.

'Where exactly are they?'

'I'm not sure,' said Bryn. 'I can't remember how we got there. All the coves look alike.'

Chapter five

'Do you think we could go over to Annet one day?' asked Bryn. 'I mean, could we land there and see the seals and birds?'

'As a matter of fact, I'm going over tomorrow morning to put out lobster pots,' said Uncle Frank, 'but I shan't be landing. Want to come for the trip?'

'Yes please,' said Bryn. He badly wanted to see Annet and there was always the chance that his uncle might change his mind and let them land.

'I'll come too,' said Sam.

'It'll have to be an early start,' said Uncle Frank.

Dawn was breaking when they reached the harbour. The sky was pale yellow as the sun rose over the islands. It promised to be another hot day.

Sam started up the engine and soon *Seafarer* was cutting through the water. Bryn, sitting in the bows, was drenched by the spray but he didn't mind. He wondered whether he might dare to ask to take over the tiller from Sam.

As though his uncle read his thoughts he said, 'It looks easy enough, Bryn, but you have to look out for submerged rocks. Where you see those dark shadows on the water and frills of white foam, that means danger.' He pointed towards the island.

'Nose her towards that cove, Sam. You'll find the tide will push her away but hold her steady.'

'What makes the tide change?' asked Bryn. He had noticed tides and currents marked on Murray's map. You had to be pretty knowledgeable to navigate these waters. There were so many hazards.

'It has to do with the pull of the moon and the sun on the sea which causes a bulge which we call the tide. The moon is closer to the earth than the sun and so its pull is greater. Then you must look out for undercurrents which can drag you on to the rocks. They're very strong.'

Bryn gave up his idea of taking the tiller. Instead, he kept his eyes skinned and hoped Sam knew what he was about.

'Make for those rocks,' said Uncle Frank. 'It's a good place for lobsters.' He took the tiller and switched off the engine, and the boat drifted gently towards a cove. 'Get hold of the oars and hold the boat steady, Sam, while I lower the pots.'

He attached each basket to a float and let it down into the water. He then told Sam to move away from the rocks while he restarted the engine.

'We've made good time,' he said. 'We'll go along the coast for a while and look for seals.'

Already the sun was high and a number of seals lay basking on the rocky ledges just above the water-line. They lifted their heads idly to watch the boat but seemed undisturbed by its passing. Through his binoculars, Bryn could see them quite clearly, even their whiskers and their gentle eyes and the glistening sheen on their coats.

They chugged on slowly towards the northern tip of the island, passing sandy coves where seabirds rose screaming, protesting at the disturbance. Bryn swept the shore with his binoculars and spotted a rowing boat on the beach.

'Look!' he shouted. 'That's Murray's boat!'

'You can't tell,' said Sam. 'It could be anyone's. Murray hardly ever comes over here.'

'Whoever it is must have had permission,' said Uncle Frank. 'We'll go on round to the other side of the island. You might be able to clock up a few more birds there, Bryn.'

They rounded the headland and continued down the coast which was patterned with promontories and inlets; a wild dangerous place.

'The *Thomas Lawson* went down here in 1907,' said Sam. 'Mark Tyler told me about it the other day. He said if you could bring up all the treasure from those old wrecks, you'd be a millionaire.'

'There's nothing left in the way of treasure,' said Uncle Frank. 'Anyone diving these days is doing it for sport, just exploring the rocks.'

'Mark's father does quite a bit. If he asks me on to his launch could I go, Dad?'

'I'd want to have a word with him first and see what he has in mind. I wouldn't want you doing any diving. That's for experts.'

'There's a launch out there now,' said Bryn. 'Almost hidden behind those islands.'

'It must be Mark's,' said Sam with excitement.

'I hope they know what they're doing,' said his father. 'It's dangerous amongst those islands even for someone with local knowledge.'

They had reached a wide bay on the south side of the island when they saw a figure walking up over the hill.

'It's Mark Tyler,' shouted Sam, waving to him. 'He must have come over in that boat we saw. He never told me he was coming over to Annet.'

The figure raised his hand in recognition and turned away over the hill.

'Neither should he,' said Uncle Frank. 'Not in that small boat. We'll go back and make sure he leaves the island.'

It was hard going against the tide and it took them a good twenty minutes to reach the cove. The boat was still in the same place, but there was no sign of Mark. Bryn took another look at it through his binoculars and this time he saw a man walking along the shore dressed in a wet suit. The next moment he moved out of sight.

'It must belong to someone else. Mark didn't have a wet suit with him,' said Sam. 'Shall we go and have a look?'

Uncle Frank was firm. 'It's not for me to turn anyone off,' he said. 'I haven't got time to go chasing people over the island. We'll report them to a warden.'

On the way back, Bryn was silent. He was pretty sure that was Murray's boat and the man in the diving suit could have been him. But how did Mark get on the island and why was he there?

Later that day, Bryn went to look for Pete. The door of his cottage stood open and Murray was on the phone. Not wanting to eavesdrop, yet uncertain whether to go in, he waited outside. Murray's voice was quite clear.

'I'm certain they're doing something illegal,' he said, 'but I haven't anything definite to go on yet. I'm keeping my eyes open and I'll be in touch as soon as I have something to report.'

Bryn didn't want Murray to think he had been

listening. He waited for a while and then knocked on the door.

'Can I come in?' he asked.

'Hullo, Bryn. Come to see Pete? He's down at the harbour.'

Murray was studying the map on the wall.

Bryn came to the point straight away. 'Are you a deep-sea diver?' he asked.

'I do a bit of it. Why?'

'Were you over on Annet today? I thought I saw your boat.'

Murray turned to look at him.

'Why this interrogation? What were you doing over there?'

'I went to lay lobster pots with Uncle Frank and then we looked for seals.'

'And did you find any?'

'Plenty. But was it you?'

Murray was thoughtful for a moment. Then he said, 'Yes, I was there. I often go and check on the island. When the water's clear I do a bit of diving.'

'Did you see anyone else there?' asked Bryn.

'No. If I had, I'd have turned them off.'

'But we did. It was Mark Tyler, the boy who was throwing stones at the seals.'

They were interrupted by the telephone ringing. Murray got up to answer it. 'I've been waiting for this call,' he said to Bryn. 'Why don't you go and find Pete?'

Bryn wandered off down the road, deeply puzzled. Something was going on that Murray didn't want him to hear. Whom did he suspect of doing something illegal?

He had reached the end of the lane when he saw Uncle Frank coming towards him.

'Hullo, Bryn. Where've you been?'

'To Pete's house but he's not there.'

'That's where I'm making for. I want to have a word with Murray about those two men we saw on Annet.'

Bryn nodded and carried on down to the fishing harbour. He found Pete bending over a rock pool.

'Hi there,' said Pete. 'Look at these urchins. Ever seen one before?'

'No,' said Bryn, giving one a poke. 'Wow. They're sharp.' Pete lifted a piece of seaweed to expose a tiny crab and some tiddlers. They watched them for a while, then Bryn said, 'I went over to Annet this morning with Uncle Frank to lay some lobster pots. We saw Mark over there.'

Pete looked up, suddenly interested. 'He's not allowed there.'

'I know. Your dad was there too but he didn't see Mark. I asked him just now.'

'What was he doing?'

'Wandering about the island. Uncle Frank's gone to talk to your dad about it. Pete, what do you think Mark was doing?'

'Dunno,' said Pete. 'Perhaps he didn't know he wasn't allowed.'

'I saw a launch out there, too. I couldn't see the name. I wonder if it belonged to Mark's father?'

'Could be,' said Pete. 'Doesn't bother me much either way.' He went back to examining the pool.

As Bryn wandered off home he gave the matter some thought. The fact that Mark had been wandering around on Annet didn't seem to worry anyone else, so why should he be so concerned about it? But then there was Murray's phone call. He seemed to think that something was going on.

Chapter six

The next day, Sam announced that he was going fishing with Mark.

'Whereabouts are you going?' asked Bryn.

'Haven't decided,' said Sam. 'Somewhere between here and Annet probably. Why?'

Bryn felt uneasy. They might well be fishing but he was pretty certain they would be on the look-out for Murray's seal enclosure. It wasn't Sam he was worried about but he didn't trust Mark. Perhaps he should speak to Pete about it.

He set off for Pete's cottage but the door was closed and everyone was out. He ran down to the harbour. Most of the fishing boats were out and there were only a few tourists wandering about. He would just have to wait till they got back.

He returned up the hill, past the church. He passed it every time he went down to the harbour but today he suddenly decided to go in and have a look. It was quiet and cool inside. Someone had put some sweetpeas in the window and the scent filled the church. He wandered round until he came to a board on which was inscribed a list of the men who had lost their lives as lifeboat crews or in the Navy. Some families had lost more than one member. The people here must have tremendous faith. Bryn thought that he would have been very angry with God for allowing them to die.

He looked at the hand-embroidered kneelers, most of them with scenes of the sea. 'For Those in Peril on the Sea' was the inscription on one, and on another, 'The Wind and Waves obey Him'.

Then he came to a brass plate set in the wall. He stopped in front of it and began to read. It was a memorial to a child of seven, the daughter of a lighthouse keeper.

He had just finished when the door opened and Murray walked in, followed by Pete.

'Hullo,' said Murray, showing no surprise at seeing him there. 'It's a good place to be on a hot day. Nice and cool.'

'I've been looking for you,' said Bryn.

'Come to mend the door,' said Murray, setting down his tools.

'Did you see the memorial to the lighthouse keeper's daughter?' asked Pete, walking down the aisle.

'I've just read it,' said Bryn. 'It was a long time ago. If I'd been the lighthouse keeper I'd expect God to make the girl better. He could have done, couldn't he, instead of letting her die so young?'

Pete was silent for a while and Bryn wished he hadn't asked. Perhaps Pete was ill enough to die, too. Perhaps he even expected to. But Pete didn't seem worried.

'God doesn't always do what we ask him,' he said, 'but he understands how we feel and he's always there to help.'

'How can you find him?' asked Bryn.

'By searching,' said Pete. 'Tell him you want to

get to know him. He will listen, you know.'

It was too simple, thought Bryn. He'd feel stupid telling someone he couldn't see about his dad.

As if in answer to Bryn's thoughts, Pete said, 'Sometimes God uses other people to listen and to help.'

Like Murray, thought Bryn. That made sense.

Murray wanted them to help him with the door. Bryn was pretty good with his hands and he knew exactly what was needed when Murray explained it to him. In no time at all the job was finished.

'Want to come and feed the seals again some time?' he asked Bryn on the way out.

'Yes please,' said Bryn.

He hung back and was glad when Pete stayed with him.

'I'm worried,' he said. 'Sam's gone fishing with Mark Tyler. I'm afraid they might find the seals.'

'Why should you worry?' asked Pete. 'They won't hurt them.'

'I don't know. Sam's all right but I'm not sure about Mark. He was throwing stones at the seal the other day.'

Pete was thoughtful.

'If they've gone fishing, they won't be looking for seals.'

'But they might,' said Bryn. 'I told Sam I had been with you to feed them though I didn't say where they were. I know Sam wanted to see them and Mark said he would take him.'

'They would never dare harm them,' said Pete. 'The entrance is padlocked anyway.'

Bryn was silent. Pete didn't understand how determined Mark was.

'Don't worry,' said Pete. 'Dad's always round

there. He'll keep an eye on them.'

'I hope you're right,' said Bryn. He felt terribly responsible.

That evening, when they were all having supper, Uncle Frank asked Sam if he'd caught any fish.

'A few,' said Sam, 'but we found the seals.'

'Where?' asked Bryn.

'Mark took me in his boat to Point Witcher.'

'You didn't get too close, did you?' asked Bryn. 'Murray doesn't like people going there. He says it upsets them.'

'He didn't mind you going, did he?' asked Sam. 'What's the harm, anyway? We didn't touch them.'

Bryn said nothing. How could he tell Sam what he could or could not do? But he was worried. He didn't trust Mark when it came to seals. For all he knew Mark might be going round there chucking stones at them.

'Did you ask Mark what he was doing on Annet yesterday?' asked Uncle Frank.

'He said he had no idea people weren't allowed there,' said Sam. 'He was just looking around.'

'I hope you put him right on that,' said Uncle Frank.

'Yes,' said Sam. 'I don't think he'll go there again.' He turned to Bryn. 'When are you going with Murray to feed the seals again?' he asked.

'I don't know,' said Bryn. This time it seemed that no harm had been done but in future he must be more careful.

It was a couple of days later before Bryn had a chance to go with Murray and Pete. His aunt had made arrangements to take him to tea with a friend but he couldn't wait to get back to the cottage in case Pete should turn up. When eventually Pete did come round, he asked Bryn if he would like to come with them early the next day.

When he got down to the harbour Murray and Pete were already there with a bucket full of mackerel. When they reached the cove, Murray swung the boat round and switched off the engine as usual and rowed in between the rocks.

Bryn immediately noticed that something was amiss. The entrance to the pen had been left open and there wasn't a seal to be seen.

'Someone's pulled down the entrance!' exclaimed Pete.

Murray jumped from the boat, leaving the boys to secure it. By the time they got to the pen Murray was searching the cave.

'What's happened?' asked Bryn. 'Where are the seals?'

Murray reappeared, his eyes blazing with anger. 'Some fool has broken the padlock and let them out.'

'But why?' asked Bryn.

'Maybe they thought they were doing them a good turn by giving them their freedom but I'd like to know how they got here. The only way is by boat.'

'Will they be all right?' asked Bryn but Murray didn't reply. He was examining a rock inside the enclosure.

'It's worse than I thought,' he said. 'Whoever it was didn't just release them. They killed them.'

'No!' said Bryn, aghast. 'But why?'

'There's a good profit in seal skins provided you're not caught. People will kill them, take their skins and sell them on the continent. The evidence is here.' He pointed to a rock.

Bryn gazed down at the blood-stains in horror. Tears filled his eyes. It was too terrible. He could almost feel the fear and agony the seals suffered as they tried to get away. How could anyone do it? He looked at Pete and saw that he was just as upset as himself.

Murray came over and put a protective arm round his son's shoulders. 'I'm sorry, boys, that you had to see this but they won't get away with it, I promise you.'

'But how did they do it?' Bryn's imagination was running riot.

Murray shook his head and went back into the cave. There he examined every nook and cranny. Still not satisfied, he came outside the enclosure and continued his search. Then he found what he was looking for. There, wedged as far as it could get under the protection of a rock, was a young seal. It snarled as Murray reached for it. Very gently, talking quietly all the time, he drew it out. It struggled in terror and snapped at him.

'Have a good look round and see if there are any more while I quieten this little fellow,' he ordered Pete. 'There's a chance a few more might have escaped.'

But a further search yielded nothing.

'We'll have to get this one back quickly or we'll lose him too,' said Murray, making for the boat. He picked up an old pullover and, wrapping it round the pup, handed it to Bryn.

'Think you can manage him? Keep your fingers away from him. He'll bite if he gets a chance.'

Bryn held the seal pup gently on his lap.

Restricted by the wrapping, it was unable to struggle. Bryn looked into its great eyes and saw fear and bewilderment there. He talked to it quietly and gradually he could feel it relax and, presently, its eyes closed.

'I can't understand it,' said Murray on the way back. 'I came to feed them yesterday evening. There was no one about then. It must have happened after that. It makes me wonder whether I was right to put them in an enclosure. Had I left them to look after themselves, weak as they were, chances are they would have perished. But then, on the other hand, they might not. In a way I feel responsible for what happened.'

Bryn didn't know what to say. He felt dreadful. If he told Murray that it was because he had talked about the seals, Murray would be furious and yet he had to. Unless he did, they might never find out that it was Mark.

'It was my fault,' he blurted out.

Murray looked at him in surprise. 'Why do you say that?'

'Because I was talking about your seals. I know I shouldn't have done but I forgot. I told my cousin. He's OK but he's friendly with Mark Tyler and he doesn't like seals. I'm sure it was him.'

'Hold on,' said Murray. 'You can't accuse someone unless you're sure about it. It's unlikely that a young lad would do something like that. He might chuck a few stones at them but he wouldn't be in the racket of killing seals.'

Relief swept over Bryn. Murray wasn't holding him responsible. In spite of his fears, perhaps it really was someone other than Mark. He desperately wanted it to be.

'The fact remains,' said Murray. 'I can't put any more there till we've found out who did it.'

'How are you going to do that?' asked Pete.

'Report it and keep my eyes open.'

'Unless we do something soon they might catch more,' said Bryn. He couldn't bear the thought.

'It must be someone who knows the island,' said Pete.

'True,' said his father, swinging the boat into harbour. 'I'll have to give it some thought. Hold on to him firmly, Bryn, while we tie up. We'll take him up to the cottage.'

Bryn was delighted that Murray allowed him to help. The pup, though young, was heavy and it was all he could do to carry him up the hill. Murray offered to take him but no one could persuade Bryn to hand over his precious burden. He felt the pup's distress as though it were his own.

He carried it all the way to the hut. Although it was hot outside, Murray lit the oil lamp and lowered it so that the pup could lie just under it. Bryn put the animal down on the clean soft straw while Murray went indoors to prepare a bottle of milk. When he came back, he squatted down beside the pup and persuaded it to drink.

'This one's suffering from shock,' he explained, 'and we must keep him warm.'

When he set the pup down it immediately backed into a corner and faced them, snarling.

'We'll leave him for a while,' said Murray. 'He's going to be all right but he'll have to learn to trust me again.'

'Has he got a name?' asked Bryn.

'How about Flipper? Now you'd better be getting back, Bryn. Your folk will be wondering what's happened to you. You can come and see Flipper another time.'

Pete walked with Bryn to the gate.

'I'm sure it's someone who knows Gugh Island,' he said. 'No one else would venture into those rocky coves. I want to go over there and have a look. Will you come with me, Bryn, perhaps tomorrow?'

Bryn had to wait till evening before he saw Sam.

'Someone has killed Murray's seals,' said Bryn, looking hard at him.

Sam's head jerked up. There was no mistaking the shock on his face. 'Whoever did that?' he demanded.

'Murray doesn't know. It must have happened last night. They were all right when he went to feed them. You showed Mark where they were, didn't you, Sam?' Bryn couldn't keep the accusation out of his voice.

'Are you suggesting ... ?' Sam began.

'Hold on a minute, Bryn,' his uncle interrupted. 'That's a serious accusation. Unless you have proof, you have no business to jump to conclusions like that.'

Aunt Millie sprang to Bryn's defence. 'It's understandable, Frank. He's upset, poor lad. It was a terrible thing to witness.'

'Nonetheless, we must keep calm. No one will get away with something like that and Murray will make sure that the right person's convicted but it might take time.'

'Just the same,' said Bryn, near tears, 'I wish you had never taken Mark there, Sam. He hates seals!'

46

Chapter seven

'Could I go over to Gugh Island with Pete today?'
Bryn asked his aunt after breakfast.

'I don't think you should go alone,' said Aunt
Millie. 'Sam, you could go too, couldn't you?'

'I'm going all-night-fishing with Dad and the
crew. We've got to get the trawler ready and then
Dad said I should get some sleep.' Sam looked at
his father for confirmation.

'They'll be all right,' said Uncle Frank. 'Can't
come to no harm. Just watch the tide and get back
across the sandbank by seven or you'll be stuck
over there for the night.'

'OK,' said Bryn. 'Pete often goes across. I'm
sure it'll be all right.'

'I'll pack you up a picnic then,' said Aunt Millie.

Bryn put the picnic and his binoculars and bird
book in his rucksack and went round to Pete's.

Pete was feeding Flipper with a bottle.

'How is he?' asked Bryn.

'OK. Dad says he'll survive.' The pup was disturbed by Bryn's presence and lost interest in the
bottle. It took Pete a little while to persuade it to
drink again. Then he said, 'Bryn, I think we should
go over to Gugh today and see if we can find out

anything. Will you be allowed?'

'I'm all ready,' said Bryn, grinning.

'Just wait till I grab something to eat and we'll be off then. Dad's out all day and Mum's going to a meeting. Couldn't be better. I'll leave you to make friends with Flipper while I tell Mum.'

Bryn sat there in the straw, talking to the seal. It stayed close to him as though glad of the company. Bryn hardly dared to move. This was the most wonderful thing that had ever happened to him. To have a wild creature trust him like this. What sort of person would dare to harm them?

He wondered if Murray had found out anything yet. He got up, taking care not to make any sudden movement, and went into the cottage. Murray was sitting at a table studying a map.

'A navigational map,' said Murray, seeing Bryn peering at it. 'Shows submerged rocks, depths of water, sunken ships, that sort of thing.'

Bryn had something else on his mind.

'Do you think those people are killing other seals besides yours?' he asked.

'Wouldn't be surprised.'

'But how would they catch them?'

'At night, or when they're basking on the rocks. Could even set traps for them.'

'What about when they're swimming?'

'You'd never get near them under the water. They're so quick.'

'Not even if you dived after them?'

'You don't catch them that way,' said Murray.

If, as Bryn believed, Mark had something to do with the disappearance of the seals, why was he so interested in diving? There seemed to be no connection.

'Don't worry, Bryn. I doubt they'll catch any more. The younger the seal, the more valuable is its skin and the easier it is to catch. The seals won't start breeding again till October and last year's pups are well able to look after themselves.'

'When are you going to put Flipper back?' asked Bryn.

'I can't keep him in the hut much longer. He needs the sea.'

'But not until you've found out who did it?'

'Right,' said Murray. 'Let's hope it won't take too long. If they're still around, and I believe they are, we'll find them.'

Crossing over to Gugh Island was no problem. The tide was out and the boys walked across the sandbank without getting their trainers wet.

'Let's walk right round the island,' said Pete, 'keeping as close as we can to the sea. There are a number of caves round there. I've seen them from the boat.'

They picked up their rucksacks and followed the rocky shore till they were stopped by high boulders. There was no possible way round them and they followed a path up the hill.

'That's Point Witcher,' said Pete, looking over the steep cliff. 'You can see from here where Dad kept the seals.'

'And where the fence was broken down. Pete, the only way to reach it is by sea, so you'd have to have a boat. It must be someone who lives here.'

'Or staying here on holiday,' said Pete. 'But, anyway, someone who knows their way around.'

'Mark,' said Bryn.

'Could be, but I don't think he'd have the nerve.

More likely men.'

'And they must have done something with those seals,' said Bryn. 'Your dad said they take the skins so they must have hidden them somewhere.'

'We'll have a look after lunch. I'm hungry.'

'I bet a lot of smuggling went on round here in the old days,' said Pete, biting into a sandwich. 'Plenty of places to hide the loot.'

'But where would they get rid of it?' asked Bryn. 'Uncle Frank said the people who lived on these islands were very poor. They couldn't afford to buy anything except food, and they grew most of that themselves.'

'They'd have boats waiting to take it to the mainland or over to France,' said Pete. 'I bet, in those days, the islanders found some of those hiding places and helped themselves to the goodies.'

'Do you think they smuggle stuff from abroad these days and hide it?' asked Bryn. 'I've seen it on television. Drugs and things.'

'Not here,' said Pete. 'They'd land it somewhere in Cornwall where they can get it away quickly. They have to be careful, you know. The coast-guards are on the lookout all the time for that sort of thing. They catch a lot of them but I bet a lot more gets through.'

'This would be a good place to operate from,' said Bryn. 'There's no one about, and they could take it by boat. There might even be something hidden along this coast.'

'Come on,' said Pete. 'Let's have a look.'

Bryn spotted the cave first. He thought it was solid cliff, but then he noticed a small entrance, almost hidden by a rock. When he pointed it out, Pete went ahead and disappeared inside.

'Someone's keeping a lot of stuff in here,' he called out. 'There's diving equipment and oxygen cylinders. I wonder who it belongs to?'

'And food,' said Bryn, going in after him. 'Look at all those cans.'

'Probably being used by a fisherman,' said Pete.

Bryn was already examining the back of the cave. 'It seems as though it goes back quite a way,' he said. 'I'm going to have a look.'

His eyes were becoming accustomed to the dark and he could now see a crevice about a metre high and half a metre wide. He had to double up to get in and then it suddenly narrowed. After a few minutes, he reappeared.

'Nothing there,' he said. 'It only goes back a few yards. You can't even stand up in it.'

'We'd better move on,' said Pete. 'We don't want to be seen snooping around here.'

Then they heard the noise of an outboard motor.

'What are we going to do?' asked Bryn. 'We'll be seen if we try and leave now.'

The outboard had been switched off and they could hear men's voices. It sounded as though metal and heavy things were being unloaded.

'We'd better hide,' said Pete. 'Let's squeeze into the crevice. We might find out something useful.'

There was just room for the two of them squatting down, but if anyone looked in they would be seen immediately.

'We'd better make ourselves comfortable,' said Pete. 'We might be stuck here for a while.'

'What about the tide?' asked Bryn.

'I can't see the time,' said Pete. 'Last time I looked it was five-thirty. It will take us about half an hour to get to the sandbank, so I reckon we've got about three-quarters of an hour.'

Bryn put up his hand. 'Ssh. Someone's coming.'

They heard someone moving about the cave. Bryn, from his place on the floor of the crevice, could peer out, and occasionally caught sight of a tall man moving things around in the cave. Then someone else came in, carrying a load of stuff.

'I'll put this lot just inside the entrance so it's easy to get at.' Bryn would recognise that voice anywhere. It was Mark's.

Then he got a whiff of petrol and another smell. Like rotting fish, he thought.

'We've got to get the rest of the stuff down here,' said Mark.

'That can wait till tomorrow,' said his companion. Bryn caught a glimpse of a bald-headed man.

'We've got to get these skins hung up to dry,' said Mark. 'If they're left in a pile they'll rot.'

'Sooner we get rid of that lot the better,' said his companion. 'The stench will give us away.'

'It'll wear off,' said Mark. 'I've treated them already so they'll be all right.'

'You'll not be getting any more, I hope?'

'I don't know,' said Mark. 'They're worth a lot.'

'They don't make good travelling companions,' said the older fellow. 'I didn't bargain for that when I joined the crew.'

'You won't be complaining when my dad's finished this operation,' said Mark. 'He'll see that you get your share.'

Bryn was getting anxious about the time. The tide wasn't going to wait for anyone.

Then, at last, everything seemed to be to Mark's satisfaction.

'We'd best get moving,' he said. 'The others will

be back soon.'

They left the cave and, a short time later, the boys heard the outboard motor start up. Cautiously, they emerged from their hiding place.

Pete looked at his watch. 'It's half-past six,' he said. 'We'll have to hurry.'

Bryn didn't hear. He was looking at the skins hanging from poles in the cave.

'Look here!' he said. 'If only your dad was here.'

'So you were right,' said Pete. 'It's Mark Tyler. I can't believe it.'

'I can,' said Bryn.

'You'll have to go on,' said Pete. 'I shan't be able to make it in time but you'll have to get across the sandbank and let them know about this. I'll be all right here.'

'I'm not going without you,' said Bryn. 'I'll help you along.'

It wasn't till they started to climb the hill that Bryn realised how long it would take them. Pete was all right on level ground or scrambling over rocks, but when it came to hill-climbing he had to take it very slowly. His chest hurt as he gasped for breath and he had to keep stopping. Although he tried to persuade Bryn to go ahead, Bryn felt it wouldn't be right to leave him alone.

At last they topped the brow of the hill and looked across to St Agnes. The water was already racing over the sandbank.

'We can't make it,' said Pete. 'It would be too dangerous to try.'

So near and yet so far. They could see Bryn's cottage from here but they were truly stranded on the island. There was no safe way across and not a boat in sight. They were stuck here for the night.

Chapter eight

'What do we do now?' asked Bryn. 'Uncle Frank's gone fishing and he and Sam won't be back till morning. He can't come and get us.'

'We'll have to wait and hope that a boat turns up,' said Pete, 'though I doubt if they'd get over with this tide against them. We'll just have to spend the night here.'

'I'm not so worried about that,' said Bryn. 'It's not cold and we've still got some biscuits and water left, but we've got to let your dad know about those skins.'

Pete was thoughtful. 'I wonder where Mark keeps his boat,' he said.

'In the harbour?' suggested Bryn.

'Wait a minute,' said Pete. 'There's an old cottage on Gugh. It's usually empty but sometimes they let it out to people on holiday. We might be able to phone.'

They picked up their rucksacks and retraced their steps over the hill to the cottage.

It looked empty. The blinds were drawn and there was no one about but then they heard noises coming from the yard. They moved closer as someone came round the corner of the cottage.

'Mark!' said Bryn. 'So this is where they live.'

'He might take us across in his boat,' said Pete. 'Let's ask him.'

'Let's ask if we can use the phone first,' said Bryn.

'But not a word about seeing him in the cave,' warned Pete. 'We know nothing about the seal skins, remember. He mustn't know we suspect anything.'

Mark had seen them and stood there, surprise and anger on his face. 'What are you doing here?' he demanded.

'We missed the tide and we can't get back to St Agnes,' Bryn explained. 'We didn't expect to see you here.'

Pete chipped in. 'We were exploring the island,' he said. 'Could we use your phone?'

'It's out of order. You're not allowed here anyway,' said Mark.

'Gugh isn't private,' protested Pete. 'I've been here plenty of times. Anyone can come here.'

'Not now they can't,' said Mark. 'My father rented the island along with the cottage and he won't allow anyone here.'

Bryn didn't think it was true but he wasn't sure enough to argue. All he was interested in at the moment was getting back home for a meal and a bed for the night. 'We'll go,' he said, 'if we can get back. Have you got a boat?'

'My father's using it,' said Mark. 'He needs it to get ashore from the launch. You'll have to find some other way.'

'There is no other way,' said Pete. 'Couldn't we wait till your father comes back and perhaps he would take us across? It wouldn't take long.'

'You don't know my father,' said Mark. 'If he

found you here, you'd be in real trouble. Listen, I can hear them coming up the path now.' He sounded really agitated, and now Bryn could hear men's voices not far away.

'Come with me,' said Mark. 'You can hide in that shed and I'll bring you something to eat later.'

The boys didn't argue but followed him to the shed. Mark pushed them inside and closed the door. They heard the bolt drawn across.

'He's locked us in,' said Bryn.

'He's really scared of his father,' said Pete. 'I reckon he'll come back later and let us out when it's safe.'

'I don't know,' said Bryn. 'I think there's more to this than we think. They don't need all that diving gear to catch seals.'

Pete tried the door. It was almost dark now. There were no windows in the shed but it was a broken-down sort of building and they could see a chink of light between the boards. Just then they heard the telephone ringing.

'So it does work,' said Pete. 'Looks like you're right. We'll have to stay here until they let us out.'

'That might never happen,' said Bryn. He hadn't considered this before and the thought was terrifying. These men were ruthless. They could be left to die here, suffocate or starve or something. 'What are we going to do?' he asked.

'Pray,' said Pete calmly.

He closed his eyes and was quiet for a moment, and then he said, 'Lord Jesus, maybe we were asking for trouble coming here but you know we had to find out what happened to those seals. Please show us some way out of this.'

Bryn couldn't really believe that the door would suddenly open and they would walk free. Nevertheless he found a curious comfort in Pete's faith that help would be forthcoming.

Pete was sitting on the floor and using his rucksack for a pillow against the wall. Bryn sat down beside him and presently drifted off to sleep.

He was awoken by a scratching sound. Pete was fiddling with some boards at the back of the shed and he had already removed a couple. The first light of dawn came into the shed.

'Boards are rotten,' said Pete. 'We can get out this way. Come and help me rip them out but don't make too much noise about it.'

In a few moments they had made a gap through which they could squeeze. Pete looked at his watch.

'Five-thirty,' he said. 'Another hour before we can safely cross the sandbank.' He looked towards the cottage. 'No one about yet. Let's have a look and see where the launch is. We can give the cottage a wide berth so we won't be seen.'

Bryn wasn't too keen. Now they had escaped he wanted to get home and he wasn't in any hurry to come back. Reluctantly, he followed Pete who was already scrambling down the cliff path where the men had come up the previous evening.

Pete stopped half-way down. From here they could see the cove, and riding at anchor was *The Gannet*. There seemed to be no one on board, but a dinghy had been pulled up on the beach.

'Come on,' said Pete. 'Let's get back. We've got a lot of useful information to give Dad.'

'And with any luck they'll catch them red-handed,' said Bryn with satisfaction.

When they got back to the cottage, Aunt Millie was in a terrible state.

'I've been up all night,' she said. 'Are you all right?'

Bryn was really upset. 'I'm terribly sorry, Aunt Millie. We missed the tide.'

'I guessed that, but where did you sleep? If your uncle had been here he'd have found some way of getting over to you but once it gets dark it's dangerous going round that rocky coast. I couldn't ask anyone to risk it.'

'We spent the night in a shed,' said Bryn. 'It was all right. Really it was.' It was no good telling her that they'd been locked in. She'd be frantic.

'Indeed it was not. You know about tides and you promised you would be back in time. How can I trust you if you don't listen to warnings?' Aunt Millie was near to tears.

Bryn was very fond of his Aunt Millie and he couldn't bear to see her like this. He went over and put his arms round her.

'I'm sorry. Please don't be angry with us. We found out something very important.'

'What was that?' Aunt Millie was prepared for anything now.

'You know about Murray's seals?' asked Bryn. 'We found the skins in the cave. It smelt terrible.'

'Are you sure?' asked Aunt Millie.

'They stank,' said Pete, 'but they looked like skins.'

'They had put something on them so that they wouldn't go bad,' said Bryn. 'It smelt like rotting fish.'

'But it's illegal to kill seals,' said his aunt. 'It's most unlikely that anyone would risk it. I expect they were sheep skins, something like that.'

'No,' said Bryn firmly. 'We've got to tell Murray straightaway.'

'Not before you've had something to eat,' said his aunt. She already had the frying pan on the stove and eggs and bacon sizzling. The smell was tantalising. The boys sat down at the kitchen table and Aunt Millie put the food in front of them.

'Murray isn't there,' said Aunt Millie. 'I went round last night when you missed the tide to see if he could do anything but he'd gone away for the night. As soon as you've finished you'd better hurry round and tell your mother, Pete. She's just as anxious as I am. You wait here, Bryn.'

Seething with impatience, there was nothing Bryn could do but try and read a book and wait for his uncle to come back from his fishing trip. When eventually he did get back he could throw no light on Murray's absence.

'Couldn't you do something about it, then?' Bryn asked him. 'If we don't catch the Tylers now, they'll kill more seals. I feel sure that was what Mark was doing when we saw him on Annet the other day.'

Uncle Frank shook his head. 'You're jumping to conclusions,' he said. 'It's a skilled but gruesome job killing seals and wouldn't be done in broad daylight. I don't want you getting involved in this, Bryn. You've no business to go snooping round people's cottages for whatever reason.'

'But we only wanted to use the phone, and it was working in spite of what Mark said.'

Uncle Frank ignored this. 'Just keep away from Gugh for the moment,' he said. 'Wait till Murray gets back and he'll know what to do.'

'But where is he?' asked Bryn.

Uncle Frank shrugged. 'Might be anywhere. He often goes to the other islands but he'll be back before the day's out.'

'Before the day's out!' exclaimed Bryn. 'But that might be too late.' No one seemed to be taking this seriously. Everyone knew what had happened to the seals but they didn't seem willing to tackle the problem. He couldn't wait any longer.

'I've got to see Pete,' he told his aunt and dashed out of the house before she could stop him.

By the time he reached Pete's cottage Murray was back and Pete was telling him what had happened on Gugh. He listened in silence till Pete had finished and then clarified the account with some questions which Bryn helped to answer.

'But where were you?' asked Bryn. 'They've probably got away by now.'

Murray ignored this. Instead he said, 'We shall have to get the coastguards in on this but first I want to go and have a look for myself.'

'Can we come?' asked Bryn.

Murray hesitated, and Bryn thought he was going to refuse to take them but he said, 'You'd better come along. I shall want you to show me where this cave is but right now I have a phone call to make. You go and tell your aunt where you're going, Bryn. I'll meet you two down at the harbour in ten minutes.'

They'd hardly got there when he came running down the hill.

'No time to waste,' he said. 'Everyone in the boat.' The next moment he started up the outboard and they were on their way.

'The cave's just round that headland,' said Pete.

'*The Gannet* is moored on the other side of the island, just below the cottages.'

'Do you think they can see us coming?' asked Bryn.

'They might well be expecting us,' said Murray, switching the engine to half-throttle. 'But there's nothing much they can do. They can't stop boats coming round the island and, come to that, landing on Gugh. It's not private.'

'Mark said we weren't allowed on the island because they had rented it,' said Bryn.

'Nonsense. It was his way of trying to keep you off and he wouldn't do that unless he had something to hide.'

As they rounded the headland, Pete exclaimed, 'Look! *The Gannet* has gone!'

'They'll be back,' said Murray. 'After all, they've rented the cottage.'

He switched off the engine and they sat listening for a moment. Everything was quiet except for the crashing of waves on rocks and the mournful cry of the gulls. They pulled the boat on to the beach and Pete led the way to the cave. When he reached the entrance, he turned to face them.

'They've gone,' he said. 'They've taken everything!'

'Just a minute,' said Murray, looking in. 'We've got to be sure. There might still be someone at the cottage. I'm going up to have a look. I want you to wait in the boat ready to make a quick getaway.'

Murray was back quicker than they expected. He ran down the hill and jumped into the boat.

'You're right,' he said. 'They've gone. Lock stock and barrel. They could be half-way over to France by now.'

61

Chapter nine

Bryn could not get over his disappointment. If Murray had been around when they got back from Gugh, they could have shown him proof. Now he might not even believe them.

He made up his mind that he would spend the next day on the look out for *The Gannet*. He wasn't allowed on Gugh but there was nothing to stop him roaming round St Agnes. There was just a chance that the Tylers might come back and if he, Bryn, had anything to do with it, they weren't going to get away next time.

But that evening he heard that Uncle Frank had other plans.

After supper, they were all sitting at the kitchen table playing Scrabble when he said, 'I thought we might go to Tresco tomorrow. We'll hire bikes and cycle round the island. I haven't done that for years and I'd rather enjoy it.'

'Great!' said Sam. 'I think I might come along, too.'

'Could I stay here?' asked Bryn.

Uncle Frank's bushy eyebrows shot up. 'Any particular reason?' he asked.

'No. Well, yes,' said Bryn. 'I wanted to keep a

watch out for *The Gannet*.'

'What will you do if you see her, Bryn?'

'I'll tell Murray straight away. You see, when we went with him to Gugh today, the Tylers had gone and the cottage was locked. Murray thinks they've gone over to France and taken everything with them.'

'Then it's not much good waiting around for them, is it?' asked Uncle Frank.

'Waste of time,' said Sam. 'Much more fun on Tresco.' He turned to Bryn. 'Anyway, I don't know why you've got it in for them. They use that launch for diving. Come to think of it, I haven't seen Mark about lately. He said he might take me on board and I'm still hoping.'

'Can Pete come, too?' asked Bryn.

'If his parents give the OK. Is he all right on a bike with his asthma?'

'If we don't go too fast,' said Bryn. 'I'll stay with him.'

They caught an early ferry. It was another lovely day with a stiff breeze and holiday-makers were taking advantage of it. Sailing boats and motor launches were setting off in all directions.

They got off at Tresco and followed other passengers up the hill and past the church, stopping at the shop where Uncle Frank bought them all ices. The place where they hired the bikes was just beyond the café and there they were fixed up with helmets and bikes.

'Now,' said Uncle Frank as they set off along the narrow tarmac road, 'there are no cars on the island but look out for pedestrians and bikes coming in the opposite direction. A lot of them go faster than they should. You don't have to stay together but whoever gets back to the café first, wait for the others. We can buy something to drink before we have our picnic.'

They studied the map and made for the Abbey gardens. The path was even and Pete had no difficulty in keeping up with the others. Uncle Frank brought up the rear at a more sedate pace.

They left their bikes outside and raced off through the gardens. It was a fantastic place to explore. Plants and shrubs rambled over crumbling walls, and they followed the many paths and steps which led to different levels of the old garden. Ancient pillars made wonderful backgrounds for the tropical plants and rare trees which had been brought from all over the world. They grew well in this mild island climate.

'Look!' shouted Bryn, pointing to a helicopter overhead. 'It's going to land.'

They watched as the giant machine hovered above them with roaring engines and landed on open ground only a few yards away.

'Comes over from the mainland,' said Uncle Frank. 'People come from all over the country to see the gardens here.'

A load of passengers disembarked. Bryn, idly watching, noticed a stocky figure dressed in a dark suit and carrying a briefcase. He seemed vaguely familiar but it wasn't until he came closer and Bryn heard him speak to the clerk at Reception that he recognised the deep guttural voice. He nudged Pete.

'That's Mark Tyler's father.'

Pete followed his gaze. 'Why's he dressed up like that? That chopper has come straight from Penzance. I wonder what he was doing there.'

'Doesn't really matter, does it?' said Bryn. 'The important thing is that *The Gannet* must still be around.'

It was a few moments before Tyler came out. He was alone and set off in the direction of the restaurant.

The next load of passengers was already going towards the helicopter for the return flight. Bryn, looking round for Uncle Frank, saw that he and Sam had wandered off down the path.

'We'll catch up with them later,' said Bryn. 'We must find out where Tyler's going. It doesn't look as though anyone's come to meet him.'

'Unless they're waiting for him in the restaurant,' said Pete.

'We'd better have a look.'

By the time they reached the old iron gate that divided the garden from the shop and reception area, there was a crowd of people coming from the other direction and they had to wait. When at last they managed to squeeze through and hurried to the restaurant, they found the place full and, although they checked every table, there was no sign of Tyler.

'It's no good,' sighed Bryn. 'We've lost him.'

'But we've got our bikes,' said Pete. 'We can go faster than he can and we can search the island.'

'I think,' said Bryn as they came through the shop, 'we'd better keep this to ourselves for the time being. Uncle Frank won't take it seriously and he'll try and stop us chasing after him. We'll have to give him the slip and go about this in our own way.'

'What about Sam?' asked Pete.

'We'd better tell him, I suppose.'

They found Uncle Frank with Sam at the entrance, in conversation with one of the grounds-people.

'You go on,' said Uncle Frank. 'I'll catch you up later or meet you outside the café.'

They picked up their bikes and rode off down the path. As soon as they rounded the corner, Bryn caught up with Sam.

'Did you see Tyler?' he asked. 'He got off that chopper.'

'Are you sure?' Sam looked pleased. 'So Mark's still around?'

'Exactly. They're still in the area. He must have been over to the mainland for some reason.'

'Why didn't you tell me? I wanted to have a word with Mark.'

'Pete and I tried to follow but we lost him. He got through the gate before us and disappeared,' said Bryn. 'That's the idea now. We're off to look for him.'

'We've got to,' said Pete. 'We can't let this chance go.'

'Look,' said Sam, 'if we find Tyler, I don't want you two spoiling things for me. I've got nothing against Mark, nor his father for that matter, so just be careful. Got that?'

Bryn said nothing but gave Pete a look that spoke louder than words.

Sam had pushed on ahead but Bryn slowed his pace to suit Pete. Presently Sam came racing back to them.

'There's a castle at the top of this hill,' he said. 'I'm going on to have a look at it. Wait for you there.'

The ruined castle stood as it had for hundreds of

years, guarding the Channel.

'Cromwell's Castle,' read Sam from the inscription. 'Built in 1650. You wouldn't think they needed a castle to guard this coast with all those islands and rocks around. No wonder so many ships were wrecked round here.'

'There's not a single boat in sight,' said Pete.

'But there is,' said Bryn. 'Near those islands. It's big and it's coming this way.'

'Let's have a look through your binos, Bryn.' Sam reached out for them but he had to wait while Bryn took his time. The boat was coming fast on a southerly course, about half a mile from Tresco. It was grey and Bryn could see some men on board.

'It looks as though they're in uniform,' he said, handing the glasses to Sam.

'Coastguards,' said Sam. 'They operate round here.'

'What do they do?' asked Bryn.

'Make sure everything is in order,' said Sam. 'See that no one's in trouble or smuggling anything.'

'Do you think they're looking for *The Gannet*?' asked Bryn.

Sam shrugged. 'Shouldn't think so. Why should they be interested in her even if she has got a load of seal skins? I bet they're after something much bigger. Come on. Let's follow the path across the hill. According to this map it leads back to the café. I'm hungry.'

'I think we ought to go back by the other route,' said Bryn, looking over his shoulder at the map. 'The Gannet could be moored round there.'

Sam agreed and set off at a spanking pace, back

down the hill and through a more populated part of the island. There were a number of pleasure craft on the water but nothing to hold their attention.

When they got back to the café, Uncle Frank had not yet arrived.

'Got any money?' asked Sam. 'Otherwise we'll have to wait for a drink.'

Bryn shook his head. They sat at one of the tables outside the café and idly watched the people drifting by.

'Perhaps I was dreaming,' said Bryn, 'but I could have sworn it was Tyler we saw.'

'You weren't dreaming,' said Pete. 'I saw him too, and he looked just like Mark. But I can't believe he's disappeared so quickly. He must have cut through the woods or something.'

Four men were coming along the road and, as they approached, Bryn stared in amazement. Sam let out a low whistle.

'I don't believe it,' he said, about to get to his feet. 'It's Mark.' He sat down again as the men turned into the café, deep in conversation. Mark's father had changed out of his dark suit into jeans and a T-shirt.

'What do we do now?' said Pete.

'Nothing,' said Bryn. 'They haven't noticed us. Let's wait and see what happens.'

At that moment, Uncle Frank came cycling down the road.

'Well done,' he said, getting off his bike. 'All here on time. Let's take these bikes back now.'

Glad of the opportunity to confer with him, they rode off to the cycle shop and waited impatiently for him to settle up.

'We've seen the Tylers,' said Bryn when they were walking back. 'They've just gone into the café.'

'Not on their way to France after all,' said Sam. 'They must be moored just off Tresco. I'll go and have a word with Mark.'

'No,' said Uncle Frank. 'We don't want to get involved with them.'

'Shouldn't we tell Murray?' suggested Bryn. 'He'll want to know if we've seen them and he'll tell us what to do.'

'Not a bad idea,' said Uncle Frank. 'There's a call box over there.'

'We haven't got his number,' said Bryn.

'There should be a phone book,' said Uncle Frank, fishing in his pocket for some money. 'We can but try.'

But there was no directory. Uncle Frank got through to the exchange and they gave him Murray's number. The children waited impatiently while it rang. It was a couple of minutes before Uncle Frank put the phone down. 'No reply,' he said. 'He must be out. We'll have to wait till we get back. Now let's go and get something to drink. What are you lot going to have?'

'Coke please,' they echoed.

'I'll come in with you,' said Sam.

'You'd better wait out here,' said his father. 'We'll have our picnic on that patch of grass across the road. We'll see what happens when they come out.'

'Shouldn't we tell the police?' asked Bryn. 'We might never get a chance like this again.'

'What would you suggest we tell the police if we get in touch with them?' Uncle Frank could be infuriatingly cautious.

'About the seals,' said Bryn, trying to be patient.

'We still have no proof,' said Uncle Frank reasonably. 'If we had a seal skin to show them that would be something. As it is, there is no law preventing a man from mooring his launch off Tresco and having lunch here. Now you wait here, and I'll get the drinks.'

He disappeared into the café.

They fell silent. Bryn could see his point but he felt sure that if Murray were here instead of Uncle Frank, he would do something about it.

Just then Mark came out of the café. He was on his own, and seeing them he sauntered over. Ignoring the younger two, he addressed Sam in a friendly manner.

'I've been looking for you,' he said. 'Thought we might do some fishing together some time,' he said.

Sam was about to answer but Bryn's anger was mounting. How could Mark stand there and pretend that nothing had happened?

'The last time we saw you,' he burst out, 'you locked us in that shed. We could still have been there for all you cared.'

'I did it for your own good,' said Mark calmly. 'You had no business to be in our garden. The shed was old and the door might have stuck, but it wasn't locked.'

Pete interrupted. 'And what about the seals? We saw the skins. You killed those seals.'

For a moment Mark looked uncomfortable, but the next moment he had regained his confidence and fixed Pete with a withering look, cold dislike in his green eyes.

70

'You're talking rubbish,' he said. 'Just prove it.'

At that moment, Uncle Frank joined them.

'Hullo,' he said, looking at Mark. 'Who's this young man?'

'Mark Tyler,' said Sam.

'I've heard about you.' Uncle Frank's keen blue eyes looked at him sternly. 'The deep-sea diver, isn't it?'

'That's right,' said Mark, brightening. 'I'm not an expert but I'm keen and I go down on practice dives with my father sometimes.'

'You want to be careful round these islands. There are strong underwater currents but I expect you know all about that.'

'My father does,' said Mark. 'He's very strict.'

'What are you after?' asked Uncle Frank casually.

'Wrecks,' said Mark. 'There's a fantastic number around here.'

'Most of them have been explored already,' said Uncle Frank. 'Found anything?'

Mark was about to answer when the other three men came out of the café. One of them shouted across to him.

'My father,' said Mark. 'I've got to go. See you!' and he left.

'A pity,' said Uncle Frank. 'I think we were about to get some useful information from him. I wonder where they're moored.'

'Let's follow them,' said Sam.

'No,' said Uncle Frank. 'The best thing we can do now is get back and report to Murray.'

Chapter ten

When they reached the harbour there was *The Gannet* moored alongside other yachts some distance from the quayside.

'But where are the Tylers?' asked Bryn. 'They must still be on the island.'

'Let's wait and see what happens,' said Sam.

'There's nothing we can do,' said Uncle Frank. 'Best go home. Here's the ferry coming now.'

As it left the harbour, they passed quite close to *The Gannet*. There was a man on board sweeping down the decks, but no sign of the Tylers. Bryn couldn't figure out where they had disappeared to.

'They wouldn't have moored here,' said Sam, 'in full view of everyone if they were up to something. I don't know why you suspect them.'

'Because Mark killed the seals,' said Pete, 'and we found the skins and they locked us in the shed and – ,' he was beside himself with anger and frustration, 'and they're so nasty!'

As the ferry tied up alongside the quay at St Agnes, Pete and Bryn were first off the ferry. 'We're going to find Dad,' said Pete.

'Tell him I'll be round to see him presently,' Uncle Frank shouted after them. Sam had lost interest and went over to talk to a friend who was fishing on the harbour wall.

When they reached the cottage, they found Murray on his knees feeding the seal pup.

'We've seen the Tylers!' said Pete. 'We've been trying to phone you. Where were you?'

'We've been to Tresco,' put in Bryn. 'We saw Mr Tyler get off the helicopter.'

Murray never expressed much surprise when they told him something, but now he was decidedly interested.

'Did you speak to him?' he asked.

'We spoke to Mark,' said Bryn. 'They were in the café and Mark came and talked to us. Uncle Frank asked him some questions about deep-sea diving but his father called him away. Uncle Frank's coming to see you in a minute but shouldn't we go back to Tresco right now?'

'Please Dad,' urged Pete. 'If you don't do something, they'll get away again.'

They heard the gate click and Uncle Frank walked up the path.

'I had my hands pretty full preventing these young detectives from taking matters into their own hands,' he said to Murray. He smiled at the boys. 'I think perhaps we should leave this for your dad to deal with from now on. You've done your bit.'

'But what happens now?' asked Pete.

'Now look here,' said Murray. 'I want you to listen to me. This thing is altogether bigger than you think and it's dangerous. If these people are caught, they're going to put up a fight and I don't want you around when that happens.'

'What do you mean by bigger?' asked Bryn, eyes bright with excitement.

'I think the skins, terrible though that is, are of secondary importance. They could be using that as a cover for something else. You've provided us with some useful information, and we're grateful, but from now on you could do more harm than good. You'll understand later when I explain it to you but, for now, we must leave it to the authorities. It's been reported and now all we can do is wait.'

'Murray's right,' said Uncle Frank. 'Now off you go and find something else to occupy your time.'

Disappointed, the boys turned away.

'Bryn!'

Bryn turned back.

'I shall be away tomorrow,' said Murray. 'I wonder if you and Pete would feed Flipper for me?'

Bryn sat silent with his thoughts. Every attempt by Aunt Millie to ask about their trip to Tresco met with short answers. Bryn couldn't see why Murray couldn't trust them with more information. After all, he and Pete had helped him quite a lot and what were they getting in return? Murray only wanted them out of the way.

He didn't feel like spending the evening indoors, so after supper he went outside and wandered up the hill. It was almost dark now and the lights shining from cottage windows looked cosy and welcoming. He loved this time of day on the island when the stars came out and all round him was the sound of the sea. It was like another world. These last few days he hadn't thought about his family quite so much. Somehow he didn't feel as angry as he did but he still dreaded going home.

It was hard to believe that there were people like the Tylers here using these islands for their own greedy purposes, but then the real islanders, people like Aunt Millie and Uncle Frank and Murray and Pete, would always care what happened here.

Deep in thought, he continued up the hill.

'Hi! Wait for me!' He swung round to see Pete coming up behind him. 'What are you doing, Bryn?'

'I like it when it gets dark. It's so peaceful. I wish I didn't have to go home.'

'You'll come back, won't you?'

'Yeah, s'pose so.' He picked up a stone and hurled it over the cliff. Far below he heard the plop in the sea. 'Know what I was thinking? If God is here, like you say, why does he allow people like the Tylers to spoil it?'

'He's not just here. He's everywhere.'

'Even when dreadful things happen?'

'Then more than any other time. He's where he's needed.'

'Funny. We never talk about God at home. Don't even go to church. He seems somehow – well, somehow part of your lives here.'

'Well, he is.'

'If he's so great, it can't matter to him much whether someone believes in him or not.'

'It matters a lot to him,' said Pete. 'He loves us.'

It was quite dark now. A half-moon appeared from behind the clouds and every now and then threw a path of light across the water. Standing on the top of the hill, they could just see the outline of Annet across the channel. To the south was Hellweathers, a dangerous stretch of water with submerged rocks. Beyond lay Western Rocks and Bishop Rock Lighthouse.

'Looks a bit sinister now, doesn't it?' said Bryn.

'You can understand why ships came to grief,' said Pete. 'Specially at night.'

'I wish we could explore Annet,' said Bryn. 'I bet there are some super birds there. I think Uncle Frank's forgotten that he promised he'd take me there and now there's not much time left.'

As they watched they could just make out a launch edging along the narrow strip between Annet and a cluster of islands.'

'No one in their right minds would take a launch through there at night,' said Pete. 'Not unless they were making a getaway.'

'It could be *The Gannet*,' said Bryn. 'I forgot my binos.'

'I reckon it is,' said Pete, 'but it's too far away to be sure in this light.'

The next morning, Bryn went round to help feed Flipper. The pup was learning to trust the boys and came up to them wriggling with pleasure. His big eyes shone and his whiskers twitched as he smelt the mackerel they'd brought for him.

They sat on the straw watching him devouring the fish. When he had finished he came close to Bryn and rolled over on his side. Bryn obliged by tickling his tummy.

Suddenly he said, 'I think we ought to go over to Annet.'

'How can we?' asked Pete. 'How would we get there?'

'We could ask someone to row us over.'

'But we wouldn't be allowed to land,' said Pete.

'But Uncle Frank said he would arrange it,' said Bryn, his mind full of the birds he might see. It was about his last chance. If they didn't take it he might never get there.

'And you want to know if that was The Gannet that we saw last night,' suggested Pete, grinning at him. 'I think you're right. I've a feeling they might be using Annet for their operations now they've left Gugh. If we go over there, we can find out.'

'And if they're after seals at least we can stop them,' said Bryn. 'Do you think we could borrow your father's boat?'

'Not without asking and he'd never let us go on our own.'

There seemed no solution. They talked about it all day and as they walked back to Bryn's cottage that evening after feeding Flipper, they were no nearer a decision.

Uncle Frank had just come back from a fishing expedition and greeted them at the door.

'I've made arrangements for you to go over to Annet tomorrow,' he told the boys.

Bryn couldn't believe his ears. He looked at Pete. Someone must have asked him.

'Well, come on, isn't that what you wanted?' asked Uncle Frank. 'I hadn't forgotten and you've only got a few more days. One of the wardens is going to take you over.'

Better than nothing, but not exactly what they wanted.

'The birds have finished breeding now and the seals don't start till October so it's between seasons. You can't do much harm there. He's going to drop you off and pick you up later in the day. I've asked Sam to go with you and I've given the warden my word you're a well-behaved lot and won't do anything silly, so don't let me down.'

It was too good to be true. They couldn't have asked for a better solution.

Chapter eleven

The next day the weather changed. As they crossed over to Annet a stiff breeze ruffled the water and clouds darkened the island. Only a few pleasure craft remained on the water. Most had already made for the safety of the harbour.

The warden, a lean wiry man in his fifties, stood at the cockpit, preoccupied with steering a safe course across the channel, and any questions the boys put to him were answered with grunts. Sam was in a bad mood. He had better things to do than waste a day with these two kids over on Annet. He would far rather have been down at the harbour where there was a chance of seeing Mark.

Discouraged, the two boys went outside and stood on the open deck.

'We'll be lucky if we see any birds, let alone seals,' said Pete. 'We've picked a bad day.'

'It's not altogether wasted,' said Bryn. 'At least we can check if *The Gannet*'s still there.'

'Supposing she is. What can we do about it if we're stuck here all day? We can't get word to Dad.'

And it wouldn't be much use if they could, thought Bryn. Murray wouldn't take any notice of them. But he didn't say so.

'Your cousin won't be much help, will he?' said Pete. 'I mean he's keen to go diving with Mark. He doesn't think they're doing anything illegal.'

'No,' said Bryn. 'Not unless we can prove it to him and there's not much chance of that.'

Presently they swung into the cove and the engine idled while the boys picked up their rucksacks and scrambled into the water.

'You'll be happy here for a few hours?' the warden asked. 'I've got to do the rounds of the islands otherwise I'd come and show you the birds.'

'How long are you going to be?' asked Sam.

'Be back here by five and we'll pick you up. If it isn't myself, I'll send someone. You'll take care now, won't you? Don't do anything silly.'

They assured him that they would be careful and waded ashore.

'What are we going to do now?' asked Pete. Getting to the island had been their goal and nothing further had been planned.

'Let's climb to the top of that hill,' said Sam. He was recovering his humour and seemed keen to explore. 'We'll get a good view of all the islands from there.'

They found a steep, narrow path, probably one used by wardens. As they approached, hundreds of sea-birds rose screeching. The ground here was covered with pink sea-thrift and heather interspersed with strange shaped rocks. In places, small piles of stones lay in hollows in the ground.

'Cairns,' said Sam. 'There're all sorts of legends attached to them.'

Topping the hill, they looked westwards to where the Atlantic raged over the rocks and there, partly hidden by a cluster of islands, was a launch.

'Must be *The Gannet*,' said Sam. 'No one else would be sitting out there in this swell. 'They should never be diving in this weather.'

'Perhaps they're after seals,' said Bryn.

'I don't think so,' said Sam. 'I bet they're diving and not for pleasure. They must be finding something pretty interesting out there.'

'We saw them from St Agnes the other evening, didn't we?' said Bryn, turning to Pete. 'They came across late in the evening when it was dark.'

'Why didn't you say?' demanded Sam.

'Didn't think you'd be that interested,' said Bryn with some satisfaction. It wasn't often he could give his cousin a bit of information he didn't already have. Sam gave him a withering look and focused his binoculars on the launch.

'It's *The Gannet* all right.'

'If only we had a boat,' said Pete. 'We could keep out of sight and go and have a look.'

'You couldn't go out there in this wind,' said Sam. 'You'd never get across. Wait a minute. I can see someone diving. They've just climbed off the launch and dropped into the water.'

'Is it Mark?' said Bryn.

'Idiot. How can I tell from here?' said Sam. 'He's in diving gear. Anyway, I doubt it. They wouldn't let him dive on a day like this. It can be pretty dangerous when it's windy. The water gets cloudy and you can't see anything. You could get lost down there.' He looked round. 'Did I hear voices?'

'Down there,' said Bryn. 'Someone's on the beach.'

Using the rocks for cover, they crept forward until they could see the shore below. Two men sat there talking. It was clear that they thought they had the island to themselves. A rowing boat lay on the beach and, stretched out to dry between posts, were a number of seal skins. Bryn recognised one man whom he had seen outside the café on Tresco. The other was a stranger. Straining to listen, he caught snatches of their conversation.

'I tell you,' said the older of the two, 'they're not going to come back. If the coastguards are around they won't take the risk.'

The other gave a short laugh. 'Neither will they go without us,' he said. 'We've got some valuable stuff here and they won't leave without that.'

'Then what do you say we do?' asked his companion. 'If we get caught with this lot, we'll have to take the consequences.'

'What the devil can be keeping them?' said the first. 'They said they'd be back by ten to get the stuff loaded and we'd be in France by this evening. It's midday already.'

'Better nip up the hill. We'll get a better view of the launch from there.'

Sam let out a low whistle. 'So you two were on to something,' he said. 'Come on. We'll have to run for it. I'll meet you down at the cove.'

He was away over the hill. Bryn knew he would never make it, not with Pete. Looking round for cover, he flung himself into a hollow in the heather and pulled Pete down beside him, as the men came over the hill. They stopped not far from where Bryn and Pete lay.

'Kids! What are they doing here?' said one.

'We'll have to find them,' said the other. They ran off in the direction Sam had taken.

Bryn lay wondering what to do. Below them on

the beach the men had left their things unguarded. He looked across to the islands. *The Gannet* was still there. She hadn't moved.

If they could get down to the beach unseen while the men searched the island, they might manage to get hold of one of those skins and provide Murray with the proof he needed. It was a risk but one worth taking, but they would have to move fast if they were to get away before the men returned.

Pete must have had the same idea. He was already moving from cover towards the path up which the men had come. Bryn followed him. They scrambled down the rocks to the beach. Pete went straight to the skins and while he tried to unhook one from between the posts, Bryn noticed a cave which had remained unseen from above. He dived in, and once his eyes became accustomed to the dim light he looked round.

The place had been used as a store, similar to the one they had discovered on Gugh. There was a lot of equipment, probably used on the launch, including a lifebuoy with The Gannet on it. At the back of the cave he found some thick plastic bags which were securely tied with nylon rope. Bryn felt the contents. Some kind of metal, he thought, by the clinking noise. Then he noticed a small canvas bag. It was very heavy. He could hardly lift it.

How much longer dare they stay? He went outside and listened but there was no one in sight. Pete was struggling to roll up the skin. Bryn could tell by his expression that it really upset him.

He went back into the cave and, taking out his penknife, slit open the top of the canvas bag. He delved into it and brought out a handful of coins which he carried to the light. They looked very old, encrusted with rust and verdigris. He shoved them into his pocket as he heard someone scrambling down the rocks. Pete had heard it, too, and came running into the cave. They drew back into the darkness and waited. The next moment, Sam appeared at the entrance.

'Where have they gone?' asked Bryn, emerging from his hiding place.

'Thank goodness I've found you,' said Sam. 'We haven't got long. They've gone off over the hill searching for me.'

'Look at this,' said Bryn, showing them the coins. 'This must be what they're diving for.'

Sam let out a low whistle. 'I reckon it is,' he said. 'It must be worth a fortune.'

'And,' said Bryn, showing them the bags, 'look at these. I can't get them open but it could be valuable.'

'Feels like metal plates or something,' said Sam. 'I wish we could get some of this stuff away. But how? Those men will be back any moment.'

Bryn was looking at the boat lying on the beach.

'There might be a way,' he said. The other two followed his gaze.

Then they heard men's voices. They were coming towards them along the shore.

'They've got us now,' said Sam.

'The cave,' said Pete. 'We'll have to hide in there.'

But Sam and Bryn had another idea. Already they were running down to the boat and pushing it into the water. Pete ran to help and, the next moment, they were all three afloat. By the time the men had rounded the rocks, Sam was rowing out to sea.

Chapter twelve

The men waded into the water, shaking their fists at the departing dinghy, but they were helpless. They were prisoners on the island.

Bryn gave a sigh of relief. 'I wonder what they'd have done if they'd caught us?' he said.

'Just held us there, I suppose,' said Sam, rowing hard to avoid a rock rearing out of the water. 'At least until the launch came to pick them up. Then I dread to think what might have happened. We've got to get back quickly and tell your father, Pete. This is too much for us to handle but he'll know what to do. He'll alert the coastguards.'

'He won't do anything till he has proof that they're killing seals,' said Pete. He lifted the seal-skin for Sam to see. 'And now we've got it.'

'There's more to it than that,' said Sam, grimly, pulling hard against the current.

'And I've got coins to prove it,' said Bryn.

'First we've got to get there,' muttered Sam. 'It's going to be tougher than I thought.'

'Can we make it without an engine?' asked Bryn as the waves lashed the sides of the small boat.

Sam was silent. He needed all his strength to battle against the current. 'I don't know,' he gasped, 'but we can't go back.'

'We might have to, Sam.' Pete had got hold of the bailer and was bailing out water.

'The tide's against us,' said Sam. 'Bryn, take an oar and we might make more progress.'

Bryn felt sure that if he moved the boat would capsize. It was a few moments before he could pluck up enough courage to go and sit beside Sam but even with the two of them rowing it was soon apparent that they were fighting a losing battle. They were steadily drifting away from St Agnes and were in danger of being swept on to a cluster of small rocky islands.

'If we get on to those there's nowhere to land and we could hole the boat,' said Sam. 'The best we can do is get past them and hope to be picked up.'

The sea was dark and turbulent and they were tossing about on the waves, alone and unnoticed.

Bryn was wishing fervently that he had stayed on the island no matter what happened. Sitting there a few inches above the sea with spray soaking him, he had never been so frightened in his life.

'Please God,' he whispered. 'Don't let us drown. Please help us.' But he didn't really see what God could do about it. He glanced at Pete. His eyes were closed and his lips moving. Bryn knew he was praying but with more trust than himself. He hoped that Pete had enough trust for all of them.

Now he was absolutely exhausted and knew he couldn't keep rowing much longer. His hands were blistered and his lungs felt as though they would burst. He wanted desperately to give up. But Pete was unable to help and Sam couldn't do it on his own. Somehow he had to carry on. He gritted his teeth and tried to match Sam stroke for stroke.

So engrossed were they in their predicament that they didn't notice the patrol boat until it was almost upon them. The sound of the sea smothered the low throb of the engine as it manoeuvred into position so that the small rowing boat would drift on to it. Willing hands reached down to pull them on to the ladder and up on board.

Only then did they see that it was Murray with two coastguards.

'You'd better go below and get dry,' said Murray, while one of the men tied the dinghy to the launch. Once it was secure the engines were switched to full throttle and they were under way.

Bryn sat there shivering. He was overcome with relief and gratitude. They had been saved from certain drowning. It was amazing when a moment ago there wasn't a boat in sight.

'Thank you, God,' he whispered.

The next moment, Murray came down the steps. Bryn had never seen him so angry. 'Now,' he said, 'I'm waiting for an explanation.'

Sam was the spokesperson but the other two chipped in where he missed an important bit.

'Look what I've got,' said Pete, unrolling the seal-skin.

'That reminds me,' said Bryn. He put his hand in his pocket and pulled out some coins. 'This is what we found in the cave,' he said to Murray.

Murray inspected them closely. 'You did well to bring these with you,' he said, 'but it doesn't alter the fact that you were ignorant fools to attempt that crossing in weather like this. You could have hit a rock and then it wouldn't only have been the boat that was lost. You'd have been swept out to sea and that would have been an end to it.'

Bryn could see that he was as relieved as they were but he was hiding his feelings behind anger. It was enough to silence them but soon curiosity got the better of Bryn.

'Were you looking for us?' he asked.

'No. It was pure chance that we saw you. We're on our way to *The Gannet*. As you rightly said, she's moored out on those islands beyond Annet and they're in trouble. We haven't time to go back to harbour now, so we'll have to take you with us.'

Bryn noticed that Murray was in his wet-suit.

'Are you going to dive?' asked Sam. He already seemed to have recovered from his ordeal and there was excitement in his voice.

'I might have to,' said Murray. 'They've been diving off *The Gannet* which they should never do on a day like this. The wind and tides make the water murky and the divers could be swept away from the launch even if they are using a guide rope. They got themselves into trouble and radioed for help.

As they came alongside the launch, a man stood on deck in diving gear. Bryn couldn't see who he was but as soon as he spoke he knew that he was Mark Tyler's father. He sounded desperate.

'We need help quickly,' he said. 'My son's down there. We can't get him up.'

At that moment a diver came up out of the water, holding on to the rope. He shook his head.

Murray didn't wait for explanations. Ordering the launch to be tied up alongside *The Gannet*, he crossed over and questioned Tyler on the details about the position, time and depth of Mark's dive and how long he'd been down.

'How much oxygen has he got?' he asked.

87

'Possibly another ten minutes,' said Tyler. 'I'll come down with you.'

Murray didn't argue. An oxygen cylinder was attached to him, and a line, and he was handed a torch. Then he followed Tyler into the water.

No one questioned Murray's authority but Bryn knew he was taking a big risk in diving in uncharted waters to save Mark's life. He must have known the danger yet he didn't hesitate. He needed all the help he could get but there was only one thing Bryn could do and that was to pray. Pete said God was where he was needed but you had to ask for his help, and Bryn knew there had never been a greater need in all his short life. This time he prayed knowing that he was heard. He really believed that Murray stood a better chance in God's hands than in anyone else's.

There wasn't much time but first there was something he had to tell God. 'I'm sorry that I didn't trust you before but I think I do now. Please keep Murray safe and please can you bring up Mark safely, too.' After all, if Murray was risking his life to save Mark the least he could do was to pray for him, too.

As Bryn waited, he thought about the treasure that not long ago had been so important to these men. Now it didn't matter, even though they must know that they would lose it and that they might be arrested. When someone you loved was in danger, thought Bryn, it didn't matter whether you were a criminal or just an ordinary person. You had to risk everything to save them.

Bryn wondered whether his own father would have risked his life to save him. He knew he would have done once but he wasn't sure any more. He suddenly felt desperately sorry for Tyler. He knew what it was like to lose someone you loved.

'Has the lad got a line they can follow?' asked one of the coastguards.

'Yes. That's the trouble,' said the diver who had just surfaced. 'He's got it tangled and the water isn't clear down there. We've been down several times and that's churned it up.'

'How old is he?' asked the coastguard.

'Sixteen. The boss didn't want him going down but Mark gets his way every time. He's crazy about diving.'

The minutes ticked by. Sam stood beside Bryn looking down into the dark water below. Then suddenly there was a shout as Murray re-emerged, bringing up with him the unconscious Mark. His father came out after them.

'Will he be all right?' he asked, bending over his son and lifting off his helmet.

They laid Mark on deck and loosened his diving suit. Murray took a quick look at him.

'We can't tell yet,' he said. 'We'll have to get him to the Naval unit quickly. He needs special treatment.'

He ordered the launch to go to Annet and then he got on to a mobile phone. While one of the coastguards attended to Mark, Murray stripped off his wet-suit as the two launches made their way full throttle across the water.

Once there, they threw out the anchor and lowered the dinghy, watched by the two men from the island. They laid Mark gently in the dinghy and rowed ashore. As they struggled up the hill with him, a helicopter appeared overhead and landed on the cliff top.

Chapter thirteen

The fishing harbour was swarming with people. When they saw the helicopter landing on Annet they came to find out what it was all about. Among them were the police and newspaper reporters. As the boys landed, they were surrounded and besieged with questions.

'What's happening over there, young man?' a keen-faced reporter asked Sam, thrusting a microphone under his nose. 'Someone in trouble?'

Sam was quite ready to supply the necessary information. 'One of the divers got trapped on the wreck. He's unconscious.'

This looked like a good story to the reporter. He was likely to get more out of these kids than any cagey adult.

'A wreck? Know what were they after?' he asked.

'Treasure,' said Sam, firmly. 'There's plenty of it out there if you can find it, but they won't be allowed to keep it,' he added. 'It's illegal.' He was just getting into his stride. It would be great if they quoted him in the newspapers the next day. He'd be famous. He could just imagine what his friends at school would think of him when they read about it.

'What sort of treasure?' The reporter was busy writing.

'Old coins, metal plates, that sort of thing.'

Bryn stood close by, fuming. It wasn't fair. He and Pete knew all along that these men were guilty but Sam wouldn't believe them. Now here he was getting the credit.

'Can I quote you?' asked the reporter.

'Certainly,' said Sam. 'I happen to know something about wrecks. I've been studying them.' Then he saw his father approaching and knew that his brief moment of fame was over.

It was now or never. Bryn broke in. 'It was Pete and I who saw those men first,' he said. 'We'd been watching them for some time.'

Uncle Frank had reached them.

'Back you go to the cottage,' he said. 'Your Aunt Millie's worried out of her wits.'

Aunt Millie had a special supper for them that evening and, by Bryn's request, Pete and his parents had been invited to join them. It was their last evening together and Maizie came in, bringing with her an enormous chocolate cake with Bryn's name on it.

'It's not my birthday,' he said.

'Maybe not, but Pete, Murray and I want to say we're sorry you're going and we want you to come back soon.' Maizie's pleasant face beamed at him.

'Thanks a lot,' said Bryn. 'I really want to. That's if Aunt Millie and Uncle Frank will let me?'

'And me,' added Sam. 'I think it will be great if you come back.'

Bryn grinned at him. It was more than he expected, coming from Sam.

'I'm glad the Tylers were caught before I left,'

said Bryn. 'This time tomorrow Mum will be here and I'll have to go home.'

'And not before time,' said Uncle Frank, with a grin. 'Goodness knows what you two would be up to next.'

'Just the same,' broke in Murray, 'they provided some valuable information. We had our suspicions about the Tylers, but until we actually caught them at it, we couldn't inform the police. We have a lot to thank the boys for.'

'What's going to happen now?' asked Bryn.

'They've been taken to the police station for questioning,' said Murray. 'All but the lad. He's in a pretty sorry state in Penzance hospital.'

'Will he die?' Bryn couldn't forgive Mark for killing the seals but he didn't want him to die.

'They think he'll pull through, though it's early days yet,' said Murray. 'Tyler and his mate are experienced divers but they should never have let Mark go down, not at that depth and certainly not in bad weather. He won't want to do any more diving for a while.'

'Did they find any treasure on the launch?' asked Sam.

'They brought up quite a bit,' Murray replied. 'Reason no one tried to retrieve it before was that anyone in their right mind would never risk diving there with those rocky ledges and undercurrents pulling all ways. Just the same, Tyler had done his research well and knew exactly where the wreck was. If it hadn't been for Mark getting caught up in his rope, they might have got away with it.'

'What sort of thing did they find?' asked Pete.

'Silver coins, bits of pottery and pewter mugs and plates. It was one of the older wrecks. Quite a haul really. Thanks to you finding the stuff in the cave and cutting off the men's escape route we've caught them all.' Murray fixed Bryn with a stern look. 'That's not to say that it wasn't a very dangerous thing to do and it could have ended in tragedy.'

Bryn didn't need to be told what a close shave it was. He was in no hurry to go in small boats again for a while.

'Who'll get the treasure now?' asked Sam.

'It's been put in the hands of the Receiver of Wrecks. They'll deal with it, probably put it in a museum. As for Tyler and his mates, they'll have a few questions to answer.'

Bryn pushed back his chair and went upstairs. When he came down he held out his hand and showed them his coins.

'Can I keep them, Murray? As a souvenir?'

'I'm afraid you'll have to hand them in, Bryn, but you can be sure there'll be some reward for your effort and they'll probably let you have a coin to keep. We'll see what we can do.'

'Why didn't they keep all the treasure on the launch?' Sam asked. 'Then they could have made a quick getaway.'

'Because it might be discovered there, and if it hadn't been for you finding it, Bryn, it might have remained in the cave for the Tylers to collect at some future date.'

Bryn was glad he had been able to help but there was something far more important on his mind.

'What about the seals?' he asked.

Murray looked at him sadly. 'It's too late for them,' he said, 'but at least the Tylers won't be catching any more.'

'What will happen to the skins?' asked Bryn.
'They'll probably be burnt.'

Bryn shuddered. 'What a waste.' If it hadn't been for Mark, those seals would have been released by now and swimming free. It was only fair that he should be punished.

Murray's expression was grim. 'Some folk are like that. Sick and greedy.'

'Are you a coastguard, Murray?' broke in Sam.

Murray leant back in his chair and smiled at them. 'No, but I lend them a hand from time to time. Keep a wary eye and let them know if anything suspicious is going on. Saves them keeping men on the island full time.'

'Now we can start up our seal hospital again,' said Pete, turning to his father.

'I've already done so,' said Murray. 'I've mended the fence and tomorrow I'm putting Flipper back, together with a couple of other seals the warden found today. It's those great black-backed gulls that attack them.'

'Gosh, we forgot about the warden,' said Bryn. 'Did he go back to get us?'

'He saw something was going on when the helicopter arrived,' said Uncle Frank, 'and went over to investigate. When he'd recovered from the shock of having his birds disturbed, he was quite understanding.'

That night Bryn slept deeply but the next morning he woke up with a sinking feeling in his stomach. It took him a moment to remember. It was his last day here. He'd had such a great holiday and he didn't want to go back to London with its noisy streets and lack of freedom. But worse than that he dreaded his father's absence and his mum's sadness. It affected all the family. Even the twins found excuses to get out of the house.

He ate his breakfast in silence. Then he walked to the top of the hill and looked across to Annet for the last time. Today the islands seemed shrouded in mystery, as though the events of the last few days had already receded into history, to be buried with the wrecks of long ago.

As he came down from the hill, he met Murray. 'I came to find you,' he said. 'Your aunt said you were probably up here. Pete and I are going to put the seals back. Want to come?'

Bryn hesitated only a moment. It meant another ride in the boat on a choppy sea but with Murray in charge he wouldn't miss it for anything. Together they walked down the hill.

'Feeling better about going home?' asked Murray.

'I don't want to go,' said Bryn. Suddenly he wanted to tell Murray how he had prayed when they were in that tiny boat and how amazing it seemed that Murray had turned up just then. 'I'd never prayed before,' he added.

'And your prayer was heard and answered,' said Murray gently. 'Were you really surprised?'

'Yes, but later when you went down after Mark, I asked God to look after you and Mark and I knew then that you would be all right. Pete taught me how to pray, you know.'

'Yes. I heard him telling you about Jesus. I'm glad you've learnt to trust him, Bryn.'

'I hope I'll be able to find him when I get back home. I think I'm going to need him.'

'You will,' said Murray firmly. 'It's going to be hard for you without your father but I think you're strong enough to cope, perhaps even to forgive him.'

'I could never do that!' said Bryn.

'Not immediately, perhaps, but later on you may find that you're able to. You see, Jesus forgives us when we do something wrong and he wants us to do the same for other people, no matter how much they hurt us. We all find that difficult, Bryn, but if we can, we feel much happier.'

They had reached the harbour, and Pete was waiting for them with the seals already installed in cages, but this time on a bigger boat.

It didn't take them long to reach the pen, now fixed with sturdy posts and strong wire. The tide was in and as soon as the boys released them, the seals made for the water and dived and rolled in the waves.

Bryn thought what wonderful creatures they were and how great it was that there were people like Murray and Pete who would always be there to look after them.

'When you come back, Bryn, these will have been returned to the sea and you can help us look for other injured seals,' said Pete. 'I'll write and tell you how we get on.'

Bryn felt a surge of excitement. The people here expected him back. They would be waiting for him and he felt that he belonged here now. But there was something else. He was glad he had spoken to Murray. He had a feeling that when he got back it wasn't going to be as dull as he thought. He expected some surprising things to happen.